CU00657829

Issue Five

General Editors
Ginny Baily and Sally Flint

Guest Editor
Jane Feaver

Front Cover Image
Matt Thomas

Printed by imprintdigital.net Exeter

Published 2010 Dirt Pie Press

The Editors acknowledge the support of the Creative Writing
and Arts Department at the University of Exeter.

www.riptidejournal.co.uk

ISBN 978-0-9558326-3-5

Contents

Editor's Note

R*iptide* has established itself over the last three years as one of the few respected outlets for the short story. When its founding editors, Ginny Baily and Sally Flint, asked if I would like to guest edit a volume, I was flattered and agreed to it with little thought as to what I might be taking on. It has certainly been a privilege and pleasure to work with the various writers gathered here; it has served also to renew my admiration tenfold for those two founding editors. Without their energies and dedication this magazine would simply not exist, or command, as it does, submissions of such high quality from new and established writers alike.

I didn't set out to find a theme – I was looking only for stories that grabbed and surprised me – and it is probably no more than a happy coincidence (if not a matter for psychological investigation) that a theme has emerged. One way or another, it seems to me, each of the stories here is concerned with flight:

Flight in the sense of aeroplanes, flight in the sense of escape, flight in the sense of fancy: journeys, evasion, invention. There may be turbulence. (In fact, turbulence became a requirement.) The beauty of it is that your feet need hardly leave the ground.

Jane Feaver, October 2010

Introduction

Luke Kennard

While second-marking a stack of writing portfolios I got involved in an argument with my colleague about the nature of short fiction. The debate centred around a pretty lousy story set in Elizabethan times, a decision my colleague felt scuppered the piece from the start. There is no historical short fiction.

'Hang on,' I said, 'what about—'

There probably *are* exceptions, she conceded, but why suppose you can apply subtext to Luther's excommunication? Why pretend you know what an awkward silence was like during the Industrial revolution?

'Didn't all Tudors live lives of quiet desperation?' I asked.

One, there isn't the room, and two, why would you want there to be? A short story should take the pulse of your society, present day.

I was bored and, frankly, a little hungover, so I started coming up with analogies. In a novel the entire extended families of plague doctors progress inexorably through their marriages, careers and intrigues. In a short story the GP says 'Open your mouth and go "Ah".' and then it ends.

'Just thinking about novels is making me exhausted,' I muttered.

I remembered a conversational essay by Carver in which he talks about not having the energy even to *read* novels, let alone write one. A conversation I had with my father in which he expressed surprise that short stories weren't more popular, given how busy everyone's supposed to be; surely something you can read on a single Tube journey would be an advantage? A conversation I overheard in the second hand bookshop in Crewkerne I used to work in. Two women were discussing buying a book, but when one of them leafed through it she found it was not, as she had thought, a novel, but a collection of short stories.

'Oh, I don't like them,' she said. 'Why bother getting into it when it's just going to end suddenly?'

Probably, I thought, it was the nature of endings *per se* that she didn't like: even in airport thrillers the ending tends to be more ambiguous than hero foils the drug baron, gets the girl and drives into the sunset. Here was a whole book full of endings, thus presenting the writer myriad chances to bilk her on a satisfying denouement.

'Besides,' she concluded, 'I like a book that's long enough so you forget the beginning by the time you finish it. Then you can read it again.'

When I was a child I always ascribed a kind of talismanic power to the last pages of books. Maybe I'd been conditioned by those shitty kind of stories where in the last sentence the narrator turns out to have been a pig or a spider all along, but I would read the penultimate page (whether it was *Podkayne of Mars* or *Return of the Native*) with one hand clamped firmly over the final page, as if seeing one single word of it would ruin the magic, would spoil whatever conclusive answer to the riddle, punchline or convincing justification for why I had just read the book awaited me. As if that's what an ending is.

Coming In To Land

Robert Shearman

Ladies and gentlemen –

We hope that you have taken pleasure in this Air Intercontinental Flight from Los Angeles to Paris, France. That you have enjoyed the in-flight entertainment system, that you have enjoyed our specially prepared meals and snacks. We hope that you've taken the chance to sit back, and relax – and maybe sleep as we've crossed all those time zones.

We now need to inform you that we will soon be beginning our descent into Paris. And we ask you to pay attention to the following information and act upon it accordingly.

We are currently cruising at an altitude of thirty thousand feet at an air speed of four hundred miles per hour. The time at our destination is 13.25, so do remember to change your watches if you haven't already done so. The weather looks good and with the tailwind on our side we are expecting to land in Paris approximately fifteen minutes ahead of schedule. The weather in Paris is sunny but cloudy, with a high of seventeen degrees in the afternoon, you may need to wrap up warm, there's a chill to the evening. If the weather cooperates we might get a great view of the city as we descend.

We hope that may be possible. The captain says he'll do his best. That would make it easier for everybody. It all depends upon the clouds. We're fighting these damned clouds.

We will soon be locking all toilets prior to our arrival in Paris, so this would be a good time to use the facilities if you have not yet had the occasion to do so. Go now. It's all right. We'll wait.

I'm sorry, that's all the time we have. I'm sorry. If you could all return to your seats. Yes. I'm sorry, madam. I'm sorry. Please return to your seats, and prepare for landing.

We ask that at this time you secure all baggage underneath your seat or in the overhead compartments. Please take care in storing baggage, and know that the contents of the compartments may have shifted during the flight. Please turn off all personal electronic devices, including laptops and cell phones. Smoking, of course, continues to be prohibited for the remainder of the flight, and will not be permitted until after you have cleared customs and left the terminal building. You are welcome to keep drinking alcohol. If you are the sort to find it calming, if you find it an aid rather than a hindrance to concentration.

Please make sure your seat backs and tray tables are in their full upright position. You may fasten your seatbelts or not. It's all the same to us. If you choose to fasten your seatbelt, insert the metal tab into the buckle by your side and pull on the strap until it is comfortable or secure. But many find that the seatbelts don't do any good. For some they are, if anything, a barrier. For some the seatbelts suggest their faith might be lacking.

And, ladies and gentlemen, be advised. It is all a matter of faith.

Air Intercontinental is proud of its safety measures, and our fleet has a survival rating that is one of the highest in the world. Last year an average of eighty-three per cent of all our passengers arrived securely and intact, at any one of our destinations all around the globe. Eighty-three per cent. That's not something to be sneezed at.

But we know too that faith is a personal thing. And that even with all the support and encouragement from our specially trained staff, not all our passengers are able to sustain that last effort of mental strength necessary to ensure their safe arrival. On every flight there will be those that fail. On any flight, those that will vanish from their seats. That'll disappear completely, and fade into thin air, the moment that the wheels hit the runway.

There are certain precautions that should be taken to give you the best chance that this will not happen to you.

We are arriving soon in Paris, the capital city of France. You will not land safely unless you absolutely believe in Paris. You are required to have faith in the city, in its culture, and in what it represents. In the very concept of Paris, on a philosophical level. If you have no faith that it's really there, then it won't be.

Playing upon your screens now are certain classic images of Paris to help you in your effort. The Eiffel Tower. The Mona Lisa. An old man on a bicycle waving a baguette. It is important that these be used as a focus for your concentration, and not as a replacement for actual faith itself. You need to believe in Paris, not merely the images put before you. The man on the bicycle will not be there to save you.

Some of you will be returning home to Paris. For you the ideal of Paris should be easier to hold. But be warned. Simply knowing something exists is not quite the same as having faith in it. We know tales of French couples, perhaps disillusioned with their lives, disillusioned with each other, who have lived in Montmartre for years, perhaps, who have more evidence than most of Paris' existence – and who, nonetheless, didn't make it through touchdown with all their body parts in place. Maybe they got complacent. Maybe, at the crucial moment, they took their minds off Paris altogether. But even if you've lived in the destination city of your flight and feel you've no doubts at all, we ask you still to pay attention and focus. Focus upon what your home means to you, right deep down in your soul.

Do not fall asleep or doze during the landing. Heaven knows where you might end up.

For those of you who have never even visited Paris before, your task is necessarily harder. But do not be unduly alarmed. Concentrate on what Paris means to you, too, and why you booked the ticket there to begin with. Why you paid so much money. What it was that drove you to so risk your very existence, and give such anxiety to the loved ones you've left at home, just to visit the place. There must be a strong idea of what Paris is in your heads in order for you to have done that. It doesn't matter how idealised or inaccurate, not if you truly believe in them. Faith isn't a spelling test. Just hold on to that inner Frenchiness you have, hold on to it tight, and you'll be just fine.

For those of you who have visited Paris, but have never lived or worked there, you may be in the greatest danger. You may only half remember a city you once visited when you were small. You may be hanging on to happy holiday memories from when you were a kid – that time when your Mummy and Daddy smiled at you, when they took you to that park, when they let you feed all those pigeons and eat that ice cream – are you really sure that was Paris after all? That you're not getting your holidays mixed up? Think. As you ate your choc ice, can you remember whether it was really the Eiffel Tower that was looming above you? Wasn't it just a common or garden electricity pylon? Be sure.

It is estimated that false nostalgia is responsible for most of the deaths and vanishings on transatlantic travel. False nostalgia kills.

For me, when I need to have faith in Paris, I always think of my time there with Jacques. Jacques and I walked along the Seine hand in hand. We drank Beaujolais and we smoked *Gitanes*, and he was the perfect lover, we made love right there underneath the night sky of Paris. With the sound of Paris in my ears and the smell of Paris up my nose, and yes, all those people watching, and some of them were tourists, but most of the peeping toms were Parisians through and through. And as he drove deep inside me, 'Mon Dieu!' he cried, and I squealed loud and shrill, I squealed loud so the noise would bounce off the Notre Dame, ring right round the Arc de Triomphe, all Paris could hear our rutting, and Paris delighted in it, because that's what Paris is, Paris doesn't care, Paris is a whore, I squealed like a little pig, *une cochonette*, that's what Jacques called me, I didn't know what it meant at the time, afterwards I had to look it up, frankly I was a little disappointed, 'Mon Dieu,' cried Jacques, 'cochonette, merci beaucoup!' So, as the plane descends, as we near the ground, I think of Jacques, it's the thought of Jacques I hold on to, and I think of how afterwards he held on to me, so tightly, and how his French peasant sweat tasted.

Some of you may prefer to think of the Louvre, or of croissants.

Please do your best to keep your children calm during the landing procedure. You will have seen how we distributed amongst our younger passengers at the beginning of the flight little picture books of Paris, along with simple but convincing explanations of the city's importance in commerce and the arts. Encourage them now to review this literature, and make sure for their own safety that they have not graffitied flying dragons or similar non-Parisian monsters over the illustrations. We invite you too, if you feel any doubts or weakness, to study the safety card in the seat pockets in front of you. The French translation of what to do in the event of a crash can be very reassuring.

Should the cabin experience sudden pressure loss, stay calm and listen for instructions from the cabin crew. Oxygen masks will drop down from above your seat. Place the mask over your mouth and nose. Pull the strap to tighten it. Then breathe normally. If you are travelling with children, make sure that your mask is on first before trying to help them with theirs.

Should this happen, of course, it might distract your concentration. Alongside the oxygen mask will drop a headset. Place the headset over your ears. Wiggle the toggle to adjust volume. The headset will be playing a medley of typical French music, from La Marseillaise to Jacques Brel. If you are travelling with children, make sure that your headset is playing first before trying to help them with theirs.

If you are travelling with children, there is no point trying to hold on to them. It doesn't work. It doesn't work. Believe me. I'm sorry. Believe me.

We are now beginning our final descent. We hope that you have taken pleasure in this Air Intercontinental Flight. The cabin crew have certainly taken pleasure in serving you, and we hope to see you again on another flight very soon.

I didn't mind that Jacques lied to me about being married. He kept the ring on, after all, and every time he waved to the barman for another drink he flashed it in front of my face brazenly enough. Every time he reached out to stroke my cheek. No, I just wish he hadn't given me a false address. What did he think I was going to do, stalk him? I'm a girl from Louisiana. I knew what this fling was, just a fling, right? But when I tried to visit his home, my next stopover in Paris, I found that the street he'd given me didn't even exist. That's what hurt. I never pretended it was love, not even as we were having sex, but it wasn't just *sex*, was it, there was something more to it, wasn't there? I thought so. I believed so. Yes, that's what hurt.

I wonder if his name was Jacques at all.

Landing positions.

Good luck, everyone. See you on the other side.

Oh, Jacques.

Air Intercontinental thanks you for flying with us. We always remember you have a choice.

Oh, Jacques, hold on tight, baby. Hold on, *mon brave*.

The Anniversary

Ginny Baily

To celebrate their twentieth wedding anniversary, Peter had arranged a weekend trip to the Italian lakes. Against the odds, he had managed to get them a Saturday-night table at Mercurio's in Sirmione.

'Mercurio's,' he repeated to his wife, Sylvia, in the taxi from the airport, not sure she'd taken in quite what a coup this was. 'And it's the right time of year for mushrooms.'

'Look,' she said. 'There's the pensione where we stayed on our honeymoon. It looks exactly the same.' She twisted her head round to keep her eyes on the white-washed building. 'We used to have our breakfast in that courtyard,' she said.

Peter didn't have a strong recollection of their honeymoon but his wife sometimes invested nondescript moments with an unfathomable resonance and so he dug around for a scrap of memory. 'Do you remember that trattoria? Where they served wonderful antipasti? Those little fishy things.'

'Mmh,' said Sylvia.

'I hope they have truffles at Mercurio's,' said Peter. 'I've never had the white ones. Giacomo Campione's famous for his white truffle pâté.'

'Who?' Sylvia turned to look at him.

'Giacomo Campione. Mercurio's.'

'How do you know his name?'

'Everyone knows his name darling. He's famous.' Peter gave a little laugh and caught Sylvia's hand in his so she wouldn't think he was patronising her. She turned back to the window, pressing their hands between her legs and squeezing her thighs together. He resisted the desire to extricate his trapped hand.

Peter went out for a stroll and a pipe before dinner while Sylvia finished getting ready. They'd had one of those unnerving exchanges in the bedroom and he thought it best to give her a quiet moment. Sylvia had accused him of not looking at her as if she were a woman any more. He'd patted her bottom and assured her that was exactly how he looked at her.

He'd taken up pipe-smoking as a poetic affectation in his youth and, although it was no longer an effect he coveted, he'd kept it up because it was such an uncomplicated pleasure. The beauty of nicotine addiction, as he explained to Sylvia who was always on at him to stop, is that it is an easily satisfied craving. By smoking you create the need and by smoking you meet it. As a result of his habit, his clothes were peppered with tiny almost-invisible holes where tendrils of glowing tobacco had burnt their way through like short-lived glow worms.

He wandered down through the landscaped gardens to the lake-shore and followed the path into a wooded area. As he stepped into the darker tangle of the trees, he could hear a rhythmic plop somewhere ahead as if a large fish were leaping and he began to hum 'Summertime.' He soon emerged into a clearing, a shingle beach silvered by the rising moon, where he crunched his way to the water's edge and filled his pipe. The lake waters were strangely inviting and, on a whim, he pulled off his shoes and socks and stepped in. He puffed on his pipe and stood under the darkening Italian sky, his sturdy body bathed in moonlight and his pale feet bathed in cool lake water.

He became aware that he was not alone. He could hear another's breath. He felt ludicrously vulnerable standing there as if spot-lit, in his soft bare feet. He removed his pipe and made himself turn round.

'Anyone there?' he called into the gloom in a voice pitched higher than he'd intended.

'Only me,' replied a male voice in Italian and a wiry, dark-haired boy stepped forward to the water's edge. He held a large flat stone in his hand so that Peter stepped back in alarm and the lake lapped at his trouser-bottoms.

'You speak Italian, don't you?' the young man asked. 'I heard you talking in the hotel.' Peter acknowledged that he did and the boy broke into a stream of chatter in an accent so thick that Peter had to concentrate. He was called Luciano and worked in the grounds of the hotel. He'd been skimming pebbles until Peter had disturbed him. Peter hadn't skimmed pebbles for thirty years but as he bent to explore the nearby stones, seeking out a flat oval one, as near symmetry as possible, his hands remembered what his head had nearly forgotten. The boy grinned at him encouragingly, big white teeth flashing as Peter slung his chosen stone in an uncertain arc. It landed in a lolloping triple bounce that made him chortle with pleasure. His companion spun his own pebble expertly so that it bounced seven times before sinking.

Standing side by side in the gloaming, they spun one pebble after another across the lake's surface, not speaking but laughing whenever either achieved a good score. Peter felt he was laughing in an Italian way, a rich fruity Mediterranean sound as if the surroundings had imbued him with some of their exoticism.

Suddenly he remembered he had only popped out for a pipe. 'Got to go,' he said, shaking his head and squatting to retrieve his footwear.

'Right now?'

'Yes, my wife's waiting for me.'

'You're married?' Something in the boy's tone made Peter look up but he couldn't make out his expression. The moonlight gave him a silvery aureola. He was a magic creature of the night. 'I'll walk back with you,' said the boy and held his hand out to help Peter to his feet.

'Are you sure?' Peter said, but he didn't need an answer and reached up to clasp the strong young hand. He allowed himself to be led into the wood.

When he got back Sylvia was sitting at the ornate dressing table contemplating herself in the mirror. She hardly acknowledged his arrival and the incoherent story he'd tried to cobble together about a drowning man and briars wasn't needed. He shot into the bathroom to tidy himself up, blot the ends of his sodden trousers on the fat white towels, smooth down his hair. What a nice little treat before dinner, he thought. He was hoping for truffles to round the evening off.

Sylvia coaxed loose strands of hair into place and examined the overall effect. She had on a black silk sheath under a bolero jacket, pinned at the front with a vintage silver and amber brooch. Her earrings were also amber, a present from Peter that she had gone with him to choose, amber studs set in curved shells of silver. She pressed the cold metal into her ear-lobes and traced the line of her jaw with her index finger. Amber, she believed, brought out a glow in her skin and complemented the honey tones in her hair.

Not bad, she thought. If only she could contain this twitching state of excitement. It wasn't just attributable to being in Italy. No, this carnal lust surged through her increasingly often these days. Out of the blue. She imagined it was primarily a physiological thing, her body crying out for one last go at reproduction before the change. Peter never took any hints. She was oozing pheromones and he would give her a peck on the cheek.

The pheromones she pictured as microscopic feral creatures moaning as they emanated from her, licking their swollen lips and sticking out their purple-red tongues. Peter's dutiful lovemaking, once a month if she was lucky, came nowhere near gratifying them. 'Nowhere near,' she mouthed to herself in the mirror, applying blood-red lipstick and remembering the trainee cook who'd served them at the trattoria twenty years earlier, his eyes black and rippling silver as the lake at night.

Peter and Sylvia joined the queue of customers between the palm trees that stood either side of the doorway to Mercurio's. Signor Campione himself, an imposing man with a billow of black hair, dressed in a dinner suit with a scarlet apron tied over, was greeting each diner in turn and ushering them in. Campione was famously irascible although he also had a reputation for devastating charm. On Saturdays, there was only this one sitting and there was no menu. You got what you were given. Since he had shot to fame with his television series on Italian cooking, the great and the good had clamoured to be let in, hot-footed it to this golden piazza and dutifully queued up outside, waiting to be embraced or derided, depending on Signor Campione's mood.

The man ran his eyes along the line of people and Sylvia had the feeling his gaze had lingered on her. When he took hold of her hand someone emerged from the kitchen and whispered urgently into his ear and as he listened and replied, he kept hold and she observed her own hand clasped in his much bigger one, the way his thumb was making tiny circular movements on the back and his fingers were lightly tickling her palm. She could feel the pheromones clustering, their little needy mouths crying soundlessly for more. When he turned back from the kitchen boy, he bent his lips to her hand and she felt the touch of his tongue. Then he raised his lake-dark eyes to hers and said: 'I remember you.'

Ship of Dreams

Jane Rusbridge

Selsey, West Sussex, April 1912

At night the breeze, salty and cool, slips like a fish through the open window and trails a stir of fabric as the curtains shift and I count the days since you left last Wednesday, my life stacked in trunks full and silent in the back room. I listen to the breathing sea as I did last summer

when you brought me here, where a sling of land offers the village to the sea and nets dry amongst fishing smacks and lobster creels. Beside tarred huts the fishermen grip pipes between their teeth and weave willow twigs, thick-fingered. There is no sound but my hair skimming to my waist, my bare feet on the veranda and the sea. The sea
a glassy sliding
shifts with the tide's heave and drag
mingled with the rhythm of your breath, pulling the air through into you, giving it no choice but to fill your lungs
and empty   now there is only the remembered rhythm

And I had no choice, the instant your palm in the small of my back made my skin gasp you moved away across the room while Esther admired the beading and brocade on my boots and whispered *he speculates, Clara, in Canada.* We glanced towards you standing with the men around the leaping fire and the glasses glittered and clinked on silver trays amongst the flotsam of words about the Irish, the Marlborough House set, Diaghilev's Ballets Russes, while my ears rushed hot with drowning

like the thunder of silence in my ears our first night here last summer when the wave pushed me down and under, beneath, before you reached me, hauled me up and said *we must teach you to swim.* Your arms held me, our skin slippery when the heat was amber thick, wrapped within the layers of Douglas pine of this tiny house that smells of Christmas and candles

leave off your bathing stockings you shouted as you disappeared across the lawn to the sea. I couldn't keep up, my feet astonished at the prick of grass blades, glossy spines like horsehair, and then the pebbles. *I can't without shoes* I cried after you as I saw the shattered white of the waves' foam swallow your shadow

They warned me.

A buccaneer, you throw back your head to laugh. You gave me a hatpin with a head of rolled copper gleaming like your eyes when you talk about pumps, engines, generators, and you argue with the fishermen about electric lamps in the village streets, show them a lump of ore and a reel of copper wire bending

but I like dusk and darkness outside and inside the hiss and stutter of the lamps. Sometimes I wonder about limitless plains and mountain ranges

Today our baby's hiccups jump inside me and the cottage exhales a resinous sigh easing through the grain as the walls dry and toast in the April sun. The pine shrinks and settles with sounds like twigs snapping underfoot. Now and then I think I hear the telegram boy's knock or his bicycle's spin and tick but not yet today

waiting

sleepy I dream over the sea pinks that bob beside the shoreline feathered with tamarisk, the track to the sea between two cottages either side like gatehouses

Open the Gate to Pleasure from only five pounds nineteen and sixpence the advertisement smiles from the window of Maidment's garage on the corner, *The All Steel Cycle*. You couldn't ignore it

striding into the shop your hand in your waistcoat pocket jingling sovereigns yellow money your watch chain glowing, so you bought us a Raleigh each. *Rigid Rapid Reliable* you shouted back, waving to Gus as he stood outside with the lean and tangle of bicycles, one forearm lifted to shade his eyes and watch us pedal away along the High Street towards the sea and home

Guaranteed for Life

that day our track was puddled all the way down to the

gatehouses decorated with spindles pointing skywards from the roof like park bandstands with music playing on summer night air

Come with me come. You wanted me to but the night shivered and collided and I dreamed of the harsh split of birth.

When the baby is born

Reverberations. You thumped the table top, laughed, wiped tea from your moustache with that quick scoop between thumb and forefinger, smoothed the newspaper. *Listen, Clara, listen. Sir Almroth writes about reverberation, suffragettes and women's physiological emergencies. He says the mind of a woman is always threatened with danger from the reverberations of her physiological emergencies.* Hah! *Such a difficulty for men, the excess of women.*

You stood, gazed, plunged onto the mattress dipped and swelled beneath us. *Excess.* Your lips on my neck and down, whispering *excess* across my belly domed ripe *the excess of women should mate* murmuring, your moustache springing *with their complement of men beyond* your mouth, tongue moving, and teeth *beyond the sea that is why I bring you here Clara here to mate beyond the sea*

our laughter licking

As warmth weaves into the thatch, doors thrown open to the sea, I unlace my boots, unpin my hat and let the deck chair cradle my body, waiting, wondering, Is it warm like this where you are? Are you on deck too? Quiet today: no music from our bandstand. No limbs loosened and dancing, the gramophone silent. My fingers dangle, waiting to hold your words, but the telegram boy has not yet called and the seagulls' imprints come and go like the patterns pressed by the languor of our bodies, the hairs curling on your chest against the glisten of my breasts when sleep is a glassy slide into

tilting my dreams the four funnels loom sleek and sheer cuffed with black steel like bands of mourning. They gouge the sky with shining and, as I shiver amongst the farewell embraces on the quayside, the funnels sink and blur into groynes that stalk across the sand and disappear into the sea. Barnacles crowd and cling like shuttered portholes or closing eyes

a paper flag, white star on red, flutters on a sandcastle but there are no children playing there

I wake chilled. Someone is knocking calling *Clara! Clara! Come quickly!*
warning
Come Quickly Danger

A stab of stars glittered above a glassy sea; below the surface the iceberg slipped and jagged.

Now

behind the house the sky is taut with screaming as wind scythes across fields of winter wheat rain-humped grass hawthorn shrivels as salt scalps the hedges here and there poppy petals splatter and last year's twigs protrude stark as bones the walls shift and sigh the door rips from my hand slaps back soaked my dress clings my hair seaweed streaming I gag on the wind's punch and bulk the waves' muscular swell
rise   release
grave reason to fear
the house drums with the urgent sea
reverberations
the ship collided and shivered water gushing deep below a glassy edge slicing my dreams
then and now Esther is here with *The Times The West Sussex Gazette* outside words inside wind slams the bedroom door the days unspool *the seamens' wives gather this morning in Southampton outside the offices of the White Star Line* but I cannot gather myself survivors' names dashed on the air *mainly women and children* grave reason to fear *those still unaccounted for include*
Frank
Frank

not yet guaranteed for life
too disfigured to be identified
unsinkable words scum on the tide's drag and heave the sea a smudged line the sky smeared grey the air smells like blood and nothing is here nothing anymore and I will run naked and roll on the sand daub and slather my breasts belly back buttocks rub
why don't you rest you must rest for the

baby Esther says hand on my shoulder
　　　the funeral ship left yesterday Wednesday: a week
　　　　　　　my trunks stacked full and silent as coffins
　　　　　　　　　　　Come Quickly
　　　　　　　　　　　　　　　Save Our
less than 675 souls
　　　　　　　　　　　　unsound
I won't hear won't listen my hands against my skull to shut out
the sea seethes and demands the rush cupped in blood bone
membrane the muscles of my heart pump and squeeze
　　　　　as you gathered me into the tendon and bone of your
motion I gathered you sliding deep now nothing but pebbles
heaped
　　　　　　　　　I am *sewn into a weighted sack and thrown*
disfigured

I can't be awake and hear the breathing sea nor think of the
bleak distance in the coffins stacked nor see the newspapers
flat on the table fat with greasy words floating *glory heroism
valour* printed columns lines and letters to parcel *unprecedented
disaster* noble Milton stanzas *no dispraise or blame nothing to wail*
nausea flames in my throat the baby turns against the drum of
my belly *reverberations* something slices like ice through the open
window and trails a fluid whisper of *last rites* over my ear
embalmers' touch on my　mind
　　　　　　　I am unlaced　　　unbuttoned　　　　　a weighted sack
　　　　　　　I will wail
　　　　　　　No waiting now
　　　　　　　No more
　　　　　　　No time
　　　　　　　　　　where we can be near in the distance the
lonely sea
　　　　　　　　　　　　my feet fast across the grass
my heel bones scatter over the pebbles' flint and curve my
soles swift with burning Esther's voice turns like a gull on the
wind calling *come back* the give and sink squeezing between my
toes lips of bubble and foam come and leave ripples on my
skin but my bones are hollow
　　　　　　　　　　I cast off my night-dress to
feel the waves' remembered swerve and glide as the sea gathers

me into the sinew of rise and swell below the surface a glassy
edge slices my lungs into a halt of breath while salt burns my
throat my body is held rocked surrounded now the water drags
me back to heave I dive under my skin gasps and a thunder of
silence fills my ears I stroke the water with the flat of my hands
        push   as you taught me last summer   breathe as I
learned to   pull the air in   the rhythm coming back   and
out   giving it no choice my limbs answering the muscle of
the tide's vigour and embrace swimming where the shattered
white of the waves' foam swallowed your shadow

I swim.

The Only Interesting Thing About You Is The Stories You'll Tell About Me

Matt Thorne

I first met Jack in 1996. Scotland is a drinking country and St Andrews has a pub for each inhabitant, but even here he suffered a permanent fear of running out of booze. He had that anxiety common to heavy drinkers or drug addicts: terror that the night is going to end. Once you'd let him into your room it was impossible to get rid of him; he'd keep drinking until physically unable to stand, then ball his jacket into a pillow and crash on your floor. He seemed to believe that late nights were for intense male conversation, something I'd hitherto rarely experienced. Years later when I introduced him to my wife she said he was one of the saddest men she'd ever met, but he never seemed that way to me.

Jack was at the bar when I met him, and I was struck by his delight at having found me, and his extreme physical awkwardness. He had a whole range of tics and affectations, and I never found out which were genuine and which put on for show. He claimed to be deaf in one ear, although which one was subject to change, and he used this weakness to dictate where he sat at the table, a power-play that would lead to our biggest bust-up.

'So have you met anyone else yet?' he asked me.

'From our course? Only Sam.'

'Which one's Sam?'

'Tall, skinny, black hair, American...' I waited to see if this would register. What I didn't want to tell him was that I'd run into her while formally enrolling that morning and the two of us had gone for a long walk on the beach. She kept saying how romantic she found St. Andrews and how unbelievable it seemed to her that she'd ended up here; I murmured my assent and didn't tell her that I was so geographically and meteorologically hopeless that I'd assumed the beach would be sunny all year round.

'Do you think she's any good?' he asked.

'As a writer? How would I know?'

He laughed, and then gave me a detailed appraisal of the writing ability of every student in our class. I was impressed by his quick-fire character assassination masquerading as literary criticism, but later learned that in fact he'd broken into the professor's office and read through all the other students' submissions. He'd done this to confirm to himself that he was the best author, having submitted a hundred page novella instead of one short story or a handful of poems like the rest of us. He did add that he'd been impressed by my work – mainly, he said, because he didn't understand it. I got the impression that he'd chosen me as a friend before we'd even met.

On this first night in a St. Andrews pub, Jack was dressed as he was every time I saw him afterwards, somewhere between Fred Ward as Henry Miller and a poor man's Indiana Jones. A dusty hat, strained leather jacket, cargo pants and worn hiking boots with thick red socks. It wasn't lack of money that led to him adopting this raggedy uniform, but practicality: he needed something that would keep him warm when he ended up on an arctic beach drinking supermarket whisky at three a.m.

His novella, *Uchi* (I believe he gave me a copy that first night) was an account of an intense relationship he'd had with a South African woman in the loser's paradise of Byron Bay. He had been living in New South Wales for the past five years, and gave the impression that he had rarely been in Britain since his birth. I would later learn that he was born in Reading, most of his adventures followed by a restorative period in his hometown with a self-made millionaire father he alternately adored and despised.

From that night onwards, I was the only person Jack consulted about writing. To him, the rest of the class were morons (among them two future bestsellers and an award-winning poet), our tutors washed-up hacks (we would reduce each other to painful laughter reading each other passages from one tutor's novel, something I now regret), the professor a distant and unengaged figure. But he and I were Carver and Ford, Ellis and McInerney, Amis and Barnes. It didn't matter that I didn't like any of these authors, and certainly wouldn't take them as role models, determined, then as now, to establish my own lineage; for Jack it was all about the glittering prizes, and my attempts to ignore all that were misguided.

The South African girlfriend arrived at the end of the first term. Jack had seemed much better at adapting to a long-distance relationship than I was – but it was clear when his girlfriend arrived that whatever romance had gone on between them was now over. We spent an odd weekend together, the three of us, during which I exaggerated my role as the naïve young writer overwhelmed by the romantic glamour and dramatic lives of his two older friends. As soon as she left he binned the novella for good and started working on a novel about his father, a long, complicated book called *Ambulant*, which as far as I'm aware he never finished.

As much as Jack had liked my story, he had no time for the novel I was attempting to write. I'd written the story while part of a university writing group who'd only let me submit my stories to their magazine if they included words like 'pinguitudinal', 'orchesography' and 'lullabide.' (I used to wonder what my old outsider poet friends thought of my later work, at least until I went on a website and discovered a poem referring to me as 'Thomas Long, the idiot novelist.') And since escaping their influence I'd reinvented myself as a new realist, something Jack, a biologist and poet before becoming a novelist, considered a kind of defeat. I didn't care about his criticisms, nor those of the other writers in my group: I was lost in a dream of composition. Maybe it was the lack of entertainment, or the absence of my girlfriend, but while the rest of the group struggled and stumbled, the stack of pages on my desk grew higher every day.

Jack was very curious about my girlfriend Stacy. He believed she was the inspiration for that story of mine he'd admired so much, and I worried that in fictionalising my lust I'd caused Jack to fall in love with her. Stacy was a Surrey girl with pretentions and I knew she'd be overwhelmed by his worldliness, which made me eager to keep them apart. But when it became apparent there was no way Jack was going to let me get away with his, I booked a table for three at the town's one decent restaurant, The Doll's House, and invited him along.

Stacy told me later she was shyly impressed with the way I took charge in the restaurant, but how else could I get through the evening? Jack immediately decided Stacy was the most intelligent woman he'd ever met, and used all his literary knowledge to impress her.

'Of course you know the Katherine Mansfield story...'

She shook her head, and Jack took great pleasure in relaying the plot of 'The Doll's House', which we'd studied in class the week before. Then Stacy asked him if he knew the Ibsen play and the two of them fell into a heavy conversation about the Norwegian playwright, madness, and the creative value of depression. Jack was an incredibly slow eater, and the kind of person who assumes other people's dishes are an extension of his own, as if we were in a tapas bar instead of the most expensive restaurant in town.

Normally he would get rid of any women who had come out with us around midnight, wanting his two or three hours of intense conversation with me before I went to bed, but tonight he made Stacy feel so special that we didn't get home until four, and only narrowly avoided Jack crashing in our room. And even when we did finally get to fuck on Sunday, it was sound-tracked by his rumbling voice on my answering-machine inviting us to lunch.

At the start of the New Year, I found a note pushed under my door. It was from Sam, writing about how upset she felt that our walk on the beach on that first day hadn't blossomed into a relationship. Was it her fault? Had she done something? Did I expect her to seduce me? Something had passed between us that morning, but neither of us had acted on it and I assumed it was forgotten. I wasn't interested in her: she was too skinny, and, as callow as I know this must sound (forgive me), any possible attraction had been permanently extinguished when she recited her poetry in class.

As Jack and I studiously avoided socialising with the rest of our Creative Writing class I realised she didn't know I had a girlfriend, so I could reply without offending her honour. I wrote back explaining my situation and hoped that would be the end of it. I also made a point of rapturously praising the next poem she read out in class (anatomising the pain of rejection following a walk on the beach), which baffled Jack, who took his copy home so he could study it alone and work out why I liked it.

I had other problems. Stacy's letters were keeping me awake. From the beginning of our correspondence she'd always spiced each missive with one or two troubling details, but now the letters were composed almost entirely of anxiety-inducing lines. She'd never been studious (her lack of ambition had been one of the things that had attracted me to her), but in her third year she'd lost all motivation and now spent her days in the cinema and her nights in the bar. Even the fact that she was seeing so many films angered me. In one letter she wrote that a tramp had approached her in a coffee shop and asked her for a massage; she thought this form of solicitation so charming and original that she'd taken him back to her room and pummelled his waxy flesh for an hour. Great: now everyone on her floor would think my girlfriend had shagged a homeless man. Next time she phoned I told her I couldn't cope: I needed to see her, as soon as possible.

The only complication was Jack. A fortnight alone in St. Andrews was too much for him. I suggested he make a move on Sam.

'Sam?'

'Haven't you noticed all her poems are about you?'

Jack always perked up at the possibility of a compliment. Such a blatant desire for approval brought out the sadist in me: my mother's influence taking hold. But I managed to restrain from swatting him down and instead replied, 'Who else do you think the tall, dark man is?'

'I assumed it was generic romantic waffle,' he replied, haughty once more. 'Or possibly Jesus.'

'OK,' I replied, 'she's no Sexton. But she's pretty, don't you think?'

He considered this. 'In a Karen Carpenter way, I suppose.'

I took a taxi from the station to Stacy's college. For the first time in our relationship she was excessively affectionate, embracing me the moment I entered her stairwell. We coupled in the kitchen she shared with the rest of her floor, an uncharacteristic act of exhibitionism. But over the next few days I sensed Stacy was dissatisfied. The less she seemed to like me, the more I demanded reassurance. On the day before I was due to return back to Scotland she left me alone in her rooms while she went off for a seminar. Twenty minutes later I found her diary—if her letters had troubled me, this was far worse. Page after page on her disappointment with me, detailed analysis of my deficiencies in bed, and how poorly I compared with her past partners. She'd made long lists of the many and various ways a man could turn her on, and how I'd failed to achieve any of them. Stacy even resented the fact I didn't smoke.

Over the last year Jack had frequently complained that I wasn't open with him. He believed I was holding back, but I just didn't feel things the way he did. I was still young, and confident; ten years of rejection had tenderized him. As I ran round to his hall to tell him about Stacy, my misery was tempered by excitement that I finally had something painful to share with him.

When I reached his room, Jack was in bed with Sam. He let me in and I could see her rearranging herself beneath the hemp bed linen he'd brought back from Byron Bay, delighted by the situation. I walked over to Jack's desk, which was covered with typed pages from *Ambulant*, each one almost obliterated with black ink corrections, took his chair and turned it to face them, nearly knocking over the globe he'd carried with him to every room he'd ever stayed in. Jack steadied it and handed me a coffee. 'OK, Tom, what happened?'

I stared at a photograph of Jack on the wall I hadn't noticed before—him upside down as he dived from a cliff—and started telling them about discovering Stacy's diary and the horrors I'd read there. Sam seemed delighted by these revelations, as if the pain of her past rejection was gone now she'd heard what a poor partner I'd make. But Jack surprised me. I assumed that because I'd treated him so cruelly whenever he displayed weakness he'd seize this opportunity to torment me. Instead he listened to everything I said with ecclesiastical concern and then confessed he'd had similar experiences himself.

'You have to understand, Tom,' he told me, 'women's diaries are peculiar documents. It may seem as if you're getting the unvarnished truth, but you have to realise they're often testing themselves, writing things they don't believe, just to work through their thoughts. And diaries, by their very nature, tend to be negative. I mean, you never write in a diary when you're feeling happy, do you? Really, Tom, you shouldn't take it to heart.'

His advice was good. But I couldn't accept it. When Stacy called she was furious that I had abandoned her. Full of self-righteousness, I confronted her about her diary, expecting her to apologise or come up with excuses. Instead she said she never wanted to see me again. I could deal with the break-up, but Jack refused to accept that I was fine, telling me that in trying to punish her I was only punishing myself.

'But I'm not punishing her,' I insisted, 'she dumped me.'

'Sure,' he said, 'but you gave her no choice. It's your ego. If you weren't so proud, you'd go there and beg her to take you back. But you can't. You're so competitive, it's going to ruin your life.'

I couldn't believe he was calling me competitive.

'That's not true.'

His voice became anguished. 'Oh, Tom, it is. You're competitive about writing, about women, even about getting attention in class. How can you sit there and read your novel out to everyone as if it's the most fascinating book in the world even though no one cares and it's all so empty and asinine. You're too young to be a writer, you've had no experience, you haven't been anywhere, you've got nothing to say. Maybe losing Stacy will shake you up, give you a story that feels true. Because right now, the only interesting thing about you is the stories that one day you'll tell about me.'

I didn't let Jack's taunt stop me writing, but I did wonder whether this might be true. I had no interest in becoming an adventurer, and I was allergic to the writers Jack liked, but I wondered whether my lack of experience would hold me back. Unlike the other writers on the course my novel wasn't at all autobiographical. I was saving the personal stuff for my second book, which Jack suggested was like a penniless man hiding a diamond in his back pocket.

I skipped graduation. Back then, such events were meaningless to me. Jack went: he enjoyed ceremony and his certificate was almost as important to him as a publishing contract. He got the first job he interviewed for: a dotcom start-up. This was one of the rare occasions in his life when he felt excited by his employment. The company received lots of publicity and were soon bought out by a large conglomerate who committed to giving every one of the start-up's workforce new jobs. But it didn't take Jack longer to discover his new position was an imaginary one—whatever the conglomerate liked about the start-up didn't involve him. He was locked into a three year contract and for the next few years he had to come in nine till six five days a week and sit in an empty office while they thought up things for him to do. This lack of purpose damaged his mental health and he soon became seriously depressed.

With his father's help, he successfully sued the company for two hundred thousand pounds. He used this money to fund a move to Prague, vowing to stay there until he finished a book he could sell. Every time I published a new novel I'd invite him to the launch and he always came, although he invariably found fault with the occasion, telling me how things would be different when he finally finished his magnum opus. I introduced him to all the editors and agents I had met at launch parties and he found them all hollow or ridiculous. For some reason I considered these dismissals as convincing as his criticisms of our St. Andrews classmates. My wife always wondered why I took his opinions so seriously; after all, he'd yet to publish a word. But I never lost faith that one day his talent would shame us all. In the meantime, his main correspondence with me was emailing links to websites hosting pictures of him off his head at random Euroraves.

In 2003 I received an invite to Prague from the British Council to lecture on the future of Contemporary British Fiction and arranged an invitation for him to come to the reception. He was well-received: they saw his awkwardness as the height of good manners. There had always been something of the diplomat about Jack, and before he decided the person he was talking to was an idiot he was always very polite to them. On this evening, even his off-colour jokes were considered charming.

The last time I saw Jack was at my wedding. It was a long occasion, twelve hours of drinking across three tony venues. I'd worried that he might get drunk or end up fighting some agent or publisher who'd been involved with a book he considered unworthy of print. But he was well-behaved throughout, drinking as much as he ever had but showing no sign of intoxication, even staying at the venue to help clear up after we'd left and tipping the cabbie to ensure us safe passage to the hotel where we were spending our first night as newlyweds.

Prague is Heaven and Hell to an alcoholic, Jack wrote in one of his letters to me, and it seems that being there exacerbated his problem. From the moment he arrived he avoided other Brits and concentrated on making friends with Czechs. But the intensity of his friendships always drove them away. For a while he was seeing a woman with a child and he got very attached to that little girl, which made his life difficult. When that relationship broke up, he gave up any pretence of trying to write and spent every waking moment drinking in bars.

Then one night he was mugged in the street. The attackers took his wallet and house keys. He thought they might be people he knew but was too drunk to tell. He cancelled his credit cards but before he'd changed the locks someone broke in and stole everything he owned. After this, understandably, he began to feel paranoid, worrying that he had somehow become a target: the drunken Englishman. He had always talked freely to strangers but couldn't do this any more. He no longer felt welcome. He had been making plans to leave but three nights before his plane trip home he decided to go on one last bender.

When his body was brought in for autopsy the morticians realised that he had received his injuries over a period of four days. Before he died he had broken his fingers, his ribs, and his left arm. He was discovered at the bottom of a stairwell and seemed to have been thrown down there by force. There were no witnesses and no one in the apartment block, which was a long way from his own home, would admit to knowing him. The police believed that he had carried on drinking after sustaining his injuries. Several people came forward to say they had seen him in bars during the period before his death, saying he was drunk and bleeding but that no one could persuade him to go to hospital.

I found out about Jack's death from Sam, who had given up on poetry and now wrote prize-winning works of literary fiction that easily outsold mine. She told me she'd asked Jack's father if she could go through his papers to see if there was anything she might be able to place. She had Jack's diary, where she'd read about the mugging and his recent decline, but although it was well-written it was too fractured in thought for serious publication. Sam asked me if I still had my copy of *Uchi*, or any of the pages from *Ambulant* Jack had read out in class. I'm a pack-rat but couldn't find them, although of course I easily located plenty of stories written by the rest of the writing group. I asked her if there was any sign of the great novel we'd all been waiting for and she told me there was nothing beyond a chapter outline and a few character sketches, including one that seemed based on me.

In spite of Jack's taunt, I have never thought of writing about him before, and he rarely featured in my anecdotes, but since his death I've considered nothing else. He would hate this story, there's no way it would've met his high literary expectations, but I hope that no matter what he thought of my writing, or of me, in describing our friendship I have at least given him one last chance to win favour with the world.

The Interview

Sally Flint

Gavin was glad he arrived outside Huntley's a few minutes early so he had time to roll and smoke a cigarette. He blew white rings into the winter air as he assessed the sharp lines and shut windows of the building. At precisely eight thirty he straightened his tie and went to the main door; it didn't open. The second door was locked too, but the third one released to reveal a tall woman wearing a red suit. She pushed her glasses up the bridge of her nose after examining a sheet of paper attached to her clipboard.

'Mr Ripley I presume?' The woman gave no indication she had seen his struggle getting into the building as she looked him up and down. Gavin fiddled with his tie to check it still felt central to the gap in his collar.

'Yes, Yes. Good morning.' He placed an emphasis on the word 'good' and immediately felt stupid for doing so. He held out his left hand to her so she wouldn't see the nicotine stains on the index and middle of his right fingers. Her flesh felt similar to raw chicken and despite make-up she was just as pale.

'Did you find us easily?' She wrinkled her nose as she spoke. Of course he smelt of the cigarette he'd smoked minutes ago. Ms Hurst had a scent of something citrus about her – something acidic. It had been a while since he had applied for a job, and this was the first time he had been interviewed by a woman. He forced a smile.

'Yes, yes, no problems.' She appeared not to hear his response as she studied an envelope on the reception desk. Gavin could see it was addressed to Ms Hurst – there was nothing wrong with his eyesight.

She placed the letter back on the desk and lightly drummed her fingers on top of it. She turned her back on him and tucked her clipboard under her arm.

Gavin was certain the intensive IT training he had undertaken would secure him this job.

'I use the stairs, never the lift.' Still with her back to him she beckoned him with a forefinger. Gavin didn't want to take the stairs. He'd already had to walk over five miles. The heat of the building was exacerbating his colour to that of his interviewer's clothes. Right now Ms Hurst's rear demanded his attention. As she strutted up the steps Gavin tried to fathom why she should wear such an unflattering red suit. Blue or green would be much more suited to her natural colouring. He wondered what she did to have such well-defined calf muscles. Perhaps she skated or went hiking or cycling, although she didn't look the type to get into a sweat. Perhaps she just maintained her agility by trotting up and down stairs all day. Perhaps she was just naturally fit and languished in bed on Sunday morning drinking coffee made for her by a handsome ex-convict who had repented his ways. Maybe she just liked to look like 'stop' on a traffic light and show off her legs, or maybe Ms Hurst had a thirst for danger.

When they reached the third floor Gavin felt more uncomfortable as they progressed down a long corridor of shut doors. Ms Hurst was only able to take small steps in her fitted skirt, so Gavin had to modify his gait to avoid overtaking. When she finally opened the door to her office she sat down at the desk, crossed her legs and pushed her russet hair behind her shoulders.

'Please sit Mr Ripley.' Gavin backed into the low, armless chair she signalled towards. The chair reminded him of the one he used to wait on outside his old headmaster's office. He resisted running a finger around his shirt collar as Ms Hurst's glossed lips adhered top and bottom and then separated. 'Mr Ripley, Huntleys is a friendly business and we pride ourselves on...' Gavin was losing concentration. He was trying to read the list on her clipboard. He could see Ms Hurst's next interview was at nine o' clock with a Mr Brown. 'Mr Ripley – can you tell me about your IT skills and why you think you would be suited to the job of technical support at

Huntleys?' Gavin shifted forward in his seat. A social worker had once told him that this gesture implied you were assertive and alert, but not threatening.

'Well you can see from my application form I have the relevant training for the job, and I have recently re-located to Manchester. I want to be close to friends and family,' he lied. 'I know Huntleys has a reputation as a good employer.' She sat expressionless as if she expected more, so he took a deep breath, lowered his voice and continued. 'And I want to work for a firm which offers me a chance for promotion.' He had practised various little speeches in anticipation of such questions and expected her to look impressed. Instead she was looking right past him at the open door and he could see little dots of perspiration glistening on her forehead.

'Promotion Mr Ripley – I'm sorry?' For a moment Gavin thought she was going to laugh out loud, but she arched her back and wedged some errant strands of hair behind her left ear before she continued: 'Given your record of...' The phone rang. She put her hands heavenward to suggest she was a vital cog in the machinery of Huntley's management team. 'Good morning.' She turned her chair so she was no longer facing Gavin and twisted a lock of her hair around her left forefinger. 'I'm afraid the interviews go on until eleven.' She rotated her chair so she was back looking Gavin directly in the eyes. 'Well I could spare a few minutes now.' She ended the call without saying goodbye. 'I will have to leave you for a moment. Take a look at this while I'm gone.' She passed him a leaflet titled 'Health and Safety in the Workplace' then left the office.

When the click of her kitten heels had faded Gavin threw the leaflet on the desk. He got up and looked down the corridor; there was no sign of anyone. He checked his reflection in the window and spat on the palms of his hands then flattened his hair. He undid the top button of his shirt and took some deep breaths before searching through the paper work on the desk, knowing he would be alerted of Ms Hurst's return by her noisy shoes.

The list on the clipboard showed details of four more people to be interviewed for the position of data entry clerk. Gavin banged the clipboard back down on the desk – he really needed this job – he only had £1.62 left out of his discharge money.

He started to scan the application forms and the details of each of the candidates and soon began to realise they all had more experience. He didn't know what they were doing applying for the job; they were all too highly qualified for it. He'd been stupid to listen to the probation officer who'd told him Huntleys had a policy of employing ex-offenders; it seemed to Gavin he was on the bottom of Ms Hurst's pile. The lower drawer of her desk contained stationery, a nail repair kit, a hair band and a packet of unopened stockings. In the top drawer, a muesli bar, an apple and a banana and what he recognised as an insulin pen. He'd got used to Mad Dave who he shared a cell with for four months injecting twice a day and having to monitor his blood sugar levels. Then he saw, dangling from the hook on the back of the door, Ms Hurst's handbag. He had it unzipped in a second. He'd always found women's handbags were little gems and Ms Hurst's bag was no exception. It contained a comb, make-up, tissues and all the other stuff of a well-groomed woman, and tucked inside the internal zipped pockets were various keys, a diary, credit and other bank cards, (her first name was Stephanie), twelve crisp twenty pound notes, a packet of codeine tablets and an open return train ticket to London.

Forty pounds was the amount he was given the morning he was released. The day he found out someone else had moved into his flat because he hadn't been able to pay the rent. The same day he'd been told by the housing office to go to the Salvation Army and the only help they could offer was a sleeping bag. His probation officer told him to keep positive and congratulated him on getting a suit from the charity shop on the High Street.

'All that hard work's got to pay off Gavin – you've got a brain so use it in the right way. Huntley's would be stupid not to snap you up!'

At the sound of heels Gavin checked the desk drawers were closed and Ms Hurst's handbag was correctly positioned back on the hook. He picked up the leaflet and started to read, then realised her footsteps sounded peculiarly uneven the closer she got. She staggered into the office and flopped into her chair; the wheels careered her towards the wall. If he hadn't known better, he'd have thought she was drunk.

'Sssory I need something to...' Ms Hurst lurched forward to open her desk drawer. She grabbed a bar of chocolate and clawed at the wrapper, but her hands couldn't get a grip. Gavin took the chocolate from her. She clutched the cuff of his shirt. He didn't move, but stood in her way so she could not reach any other food.

'You must have burnt up all your energy using the stairs Ms Hurst.' For a moment she pulled the face of a spoilt child in a sweet shop. As she tried to stand up he pushed her with his forefinger. She stumbled over the chair wheels before falling to the floor. He knew by her colour and rolling eyes she would soon lapse into unconsciousness if she did not eat something sugary. Somehow she managed to prop herself between the desk and the wall. Saliva seeped from the corners of her mouth and rolled under her chin. The whites of her eyes turned pink as adrenaline rushed around her body. He stood over her holding his breath. He could call an ambulance. He could just leave her for someone else to find. Her eyes closed. Her skin was as white as the paper in the printer, and he could see the blood vessels in her temples racing in time to her heartbeat. He nudged her left side with his foot.

He went back to the desk and looked at the list of interviewees on Ms Hurst's clipboard. Mr Brown would be here in fifteen minutes. He dialled his number first.

'Good morning Mr Brown. I'm ringing on behalf of Huntleys.'

'Oh right – I'm just on my way. I'll be with you shortly.'

'I'm afraid to say the vacancy has been filled, so we wanted to let you know immediately to save you an unnecessary journey.' Gavin glanced at Ms Hurst lying motionless on the floor, her mouth open.

He phoned the other three candidates who took the cancellation of their interviews surprisingly well. In a way Gavin felt he had done them a service. They would all probably get better jobs. He removed all of the other applicant's details from the clipboard. He then filled in glowing references on his own form where his referees hadn't responded, and also Ms Hurst's commentary on himself. He ended it: 'Mr Gavin Ripley – ring tomorrow – start asap.'

From Ms Hurst's desk drawer, or Stephanie as he now thought of her, he took the insulin pen and drew up the maximum dose. He used the gloves in her handbag so as not to leave fingerprints on the pen. He separated her shirt from her skirt and studied the trail of bruises of recent needles like minute rainbows across her abdomen, before pinching her flesh and pushing the needle in. A speck of blood like a tiny bead erupted on her skin as he withdrew the needle. It was the exact same colour as her suit. Gavin placed the insulin pen by Ms Hurst's right hand. He wiped everything else he had touched then took three hundred pounds and anything else that might be useful from the handbag and tucked them in his pocket alongside Ms Hurst's gloves. At eight fifty Gavin left the building without seeing anyone else.

He made sure his mobile phone was fully charged to be ready for a call from Huntleys the next morning. Ms Hurst would have been past the point of resuscitation when he left. Forensics would think she had just injected herself with too much insulin by mistake; they may even think her condition had driven her to end her own life. Mad Dave was certainly depressed by his diabetes and the worry of losing his eyesight and legs and often said he'd be better off dead.

Gavin wasn't worried; after all he had reason to be in Ms Hurst's office and deserved the job. Surely someone at Huntley's would have picked up on his favourable interview report by now. By midday his phone still hadn't rung so he dialled Huntleys.

'Good morning – sorry good afternoon. Could I speak to Ms Hurst please?'

'Who's calling please?'

'It's Gavin Ripley, Mr Gavin Ripley.'

He waited while the switchboard operator played him an electronic version of Greensleeves. He lit a cigarette and inhaled.

'Hello – Mr Ripley – this is Stephanie Hurst.' Gavin found himself sitting on the floor.

'Ms Hurst? I'm enquiring about the job, but I must have spoken to your assistant yesterday.'

He pinched the lit end of his cigarette between his thumb and forefinger.

'That wouldn't be possible. She's actually in intensive care.'

'That's awful.'

'I'm sorry Mr Ripley the job vacancy has been filled.'

Gavin put his clothes in a bag and caught the 2.15 from Manchester to London using Ms Hurst's ticket. On the train he sent Mad Dave a text: 'Things didn't work out.' Somewhere between Birmingham New Street and Paddington he threw a pair of gloves and a tie from the window. Folded in an envelope in the inside pocket of his jacket were the personal details of the other job applicants.

Camera Obscura

Wena Poon

Laura had no trouble picking him out at the small airport in Jerez de la Frontera.

'Guillermo!' she waved.

He was on the phone. He hung up right away and kissed her on both sides of her face. 'Welcome, Laura.'

'You look – '

'You have not changed.'

' – the same.'

'Liar,' he said. 'I have a better haircut now.'

'And I would do anything to get back to the weight I was when you last saw me.'

They laughed.

'Luggage?' he asked.

'This is all I have. Come on, let's go get the lens.'

They waited for their crate at the airline cargo office. He was given new forms to fill in and sighed, bending over the clipboard. She studied him curiously. He was still the same person, except his face was a little broader now, and there was a permanent wrinkle of fatigue under his eyes that she rather liked. It made him more interesting. She remembered him as a soft-spoken, pretty boy, struggling to speak English to her. He was now fluent, professional, brisk on the telephone.

When Guillermo caught her gaze, she said hastily, 'How do you say lens in Spanish?'

'Lens?' he looked surprised, handing the clipboard back to the staff. 'Lente.'

'Lente.'

A horse whinnied. Two British women came to claim their cat.

'Is he okay?' asked Guillermo, crouching and petting the cat.

The owners said it was a she. They fussed over the animal and squirted water in its dish.

'I've often wondered what would happen if I got somebody else's box in cargo,' said Laura. 'It could be a real surprise.'

'Gold bars.'

'Snakes.'

They both signed another round of pink and yellow carbon copies. She noticed that he had no rings on his fingers. They wheeled the wooden crate to where Guillermo's SUV was parked.

'The moment of truth,' he said, opening the trunk. It barely fit.

'This project is a pain,' chuckled Laura.

'You have no idea how much of a pain,' he slammed the door and opened the passenger door for her. 'But I get to see you.'

As they pulled out of the parking lot, she said, 'This is all so weird.'

'I'm okay with weird. Architects are weird.'

'You said it, pal.'

*

It was an ordinary day at the office in downtown San Francisco.

Dear Laura, it's Guillermo Diaz from Valencia. I am looking for an architect in San Francisco in a project involving University of California at Berkeley. Please email me back if you are the same Laura I knew.

She was no longer the same Laura he knew, but she emailed him back anyway.

*

They talked work on the drive to Cadiz. The urban blight along the highway gave way to the occasional grand symphony of a distant medieval town.

'I've never seen this part of Spain,' said Laura. 'It's so built up. I am always surprised when I go somewhere I've never heard of and find millions and millions of people living there.'

'You've not been back since I last saw you?'

They had met in Valencia. She was a college freshman on a foreign language exchange program. 'Nope.'

'You have not been to Spain in seventeen years?'

'Yep.'

'That's very strange to me. I've visited America. Many, many times.'

Somehow the news hurt her. She didn't know why. She was the one who broke up with him after her summer program ended. 'Well. We live in a big country. We're stubbornly monocultural and monolingual and we don't need anybody.'

'Clearly,' he grinned. 'Can you still speak?'

'Spanish? Not anymore.'

'That's too bad.'

'I think every white American has a story to tell about how they pathetically tried to learn Spanish at some point in their life, and how they failed.'

'Really.' He darted a glance at her. 'I worked in New York for a year.'

'So did I.' She named the firm.

Guillermo said he taught an urban design course in New York. 'Just for fun. I needed to use my English before I lost it completely. You see, we are also stubbornly monocultural and monolingual.'

'When were you in New York?'

'1999.'

'I was there in '99.'

'Really!'

They discovered that they had lived about two subway stops apart, and would go to the same lectures at the Urban Center on 51st and Madison.

'I still can't believe you're an architect, too,' said Laura, shaking her head. 'Why, why are people attracted to this underpaid profession? Will we never learn?'

'I don't find it surprising that we turned out to be architects, considering how we met.'

'What do you mean?'

He glanced at her again, then kept his eyes on the road.

'How did we meet?' she asked. It was a long time ago, a hot summer day. The Plaza de la Virgen near Valencia cathedral was packed with American tourists. Guillermo was a teenager, sitting with his friends at the fountain. 'Oh, I asked you to take my picture.'

He shook his head. 'No, you did not.'

'I didn't?'

'I asked *you*,' he said, looking behind him quickly, accelerating and changing lanes on the highway. 'I asked if you wanted your picture taken, because you were travelling alone.'

She laughed. 'Did you feel sorry for me?'

'No,' he said. 'I noticed your expression when you came round the corner and saw the cathedral.' He smiled at the road ahead of them. 'You had this look. You made me see the cathedral in a way I had never seen before. I immediately wanted to talk to you. So, it is not surprising that we are both architects.'

'You never told me this,' she said.

'If they had LinkedIn and Facebook in those days, I would have found you earlier,' said Guillermo quietly. 'It was a different world back then. California seemed very far away.'

Laura felt awkward and changed the subject. 'I can't wait to see this camera obscura thing.'

'I'm taking you to your hotel, then I'll take the lens to the tower. We'll see it tomorrow morning before I drive you back to the airport.'

'Why, is the tower closed?'

'I have keys. But aren't you tired?'

'I came all the way with this precious thing, I could at least see what is in that box.'

'Well, if you're up for it, I'll even install it while you're watching.'

'Perfect.'

*

'My father was an optician,' said Guillermo, after they fitted the lens. They stepped back and surveyed their handiwork. 'His whole life he fitted tiny little screws and used small instruments. He would have liked to hear that I am working with this large lens.'

Laura remembered that his father had died of cancer when Guillermo was a small boy. She struggled to remember other facts about his life. 'So how does it work?'

They were on top of Torre Tavira, an eighteenth century watchtower which was being renovated by Guillermo's firm. It was the highest point in Cadiz. He helped her down the iron scaffolding. 'There are two ropes and two levers. I was practicing with the old lens. I'll show you. First, we shut all the windows.'

They stood in complete darkness. The room smelled of new paint on old timber. Before them was a whitewashed tabletop. It was concave, like a satellite dish. It had a handle and could be raised and lowered. This was the projection screen. She looked up as a small, round trapdoor on the roof popped open and a shaft of white sunlight came in. A metallic groan and thump came from somewhere above them. Suddenly, a burst of complicated color on the white dish.

'It looks like an upside-down painting!' exclaimed Laura.

He spun the hidden mirror around so that the image was now the right side up. 'You can rotate. You can zoom in.'

'There's a bird flying across! Oh my God, it's live.'

'Of course it's live. It's not a painting. Cadiz used to be filled with watchtowers for observing ships. This is the last one standing. It's falling apart.'

'I had no idea it would be so cool.'

'Look, you can see people hanging up their washing on the roof to dry.' The clothes flapped in the wind. 'Here's the cathedral. Pigeons. Here's the beach.'

Cadiz was an ancient city crammed into a narrow strip of sand, like a pale galleon waiting to sail off to Africa if the right wind came. Laura saw ochre churches, pink townhouses, white walls, a tangerine cupola, an ocean the turquoise of an Impressionist painting. 'This is all outside right now?'

'I thought you would like it. You were so cynical when I first described it on the phone.' Guillermo pulled another rope and panned across the intricate town. 'The *camera oscura* was discovered by the Chinese. They called it a treasure box.'

'There's one in San Francisco, near the beach. I went as a kid. It wasn't very interesting.'

'Maybe you have to be older to appreciate it.'

Laura stared at the projected image. Perhaps it was the jet lag. She wanted to say she wished she wasn't leaving the next day. She wanted to confess to Guillermo all kinds of things in the dark, to tell him about the intervening years. She opened her mouth to speak but found herself encumbered by language.

'Strange,' Guillermo zoomed in on a building. 'She's still there.'

'Who?'

'See this rooftop? There's an addition on the roof terrace, an extra room. A lot of houses have those. See the young woman looking out the window?'

'Can you get any closer?'

'Yes.' He pulled a lever. 'I noticed her the first time I used the old lens. I photographed her image as a demo for the project. She's always there with her head hanging out the window.'

'She doesn't look very happy.'

In the darkness, his tone changed. 'They've taken down the laundry from the clothes line since I last took the photo. Look, you can see the door now.'

She saw what he saw. 'There's a lock on the outside.'

Guillermo moved abruptly and opened a window. Light came flooding in. The projected image grew faint. He folded his arms, tense all of a sudden. 'What do you think that's all about?'

*

'Hey!'

'*Hola.*' He was standing outside her classroom waiting for her, eating ice-cream. He gave her a cold, chocolatey kiss. She laughed as they went out into the sun-dappled street.

'I don't want to be in the picture,' he walked away abruptly when she raised her camera.

'Come back! There's an interesting façade behind you!'

'No!'

He knew the summer was coming to an end. They were eighteen. They both decided that it was better not to have so many photographs of each other. It would just make everything worse.

*

Guillermo was on the phone with someone in Spanish, sounding frustrated. Six o'clock. It was still light outside, but the streets surrounding the tower were deserted. Where was everybody?

'My boss told me to drop it,' said Guillermo grimly, tucking the phone back in his hip pocket. 'He said if we called the police, the city would be notified. Our relationship with the city council has been so bad since this project got delayed. The client might be upset. He says forget it, it's just some domestic abuse matter.'

'What a coward.'

'He's my wife's brother.'

He was married? The world tilted a little. Finally. It was a relief. He found some way of telling her, after all, without her having to ask.

Laura turned quickly to the image of the girl in the window. How far away was she? She was about sixteen or seventeen. She wore a headdress, but Laura had no idea what race or nationality she could be. She looked helpless. She disappeared and reappeared at the window, like a puppet in a Punch and Judy show. Was the danger real? Could there possibly be any misunderstanding about the lock on the door? Perhaps it was a cultural thing. Laura was notoriously thick about culture. It would be so stupid and American to go barging about 'rescuing' people.

She felt very tired all of a sudden. This was an image, a trick of the light, no more. She needed a shower. She wanted to get to the hotel. Tomorrow, this would not be her problem. She would be boarding a flight back to San Francisco. She had never understood this strange country and she should not have come back. Europe was the kind of place you visited during your student days. You don't go back there when you've grown up. It would be like Alice – the giant, malformed Alice – trying to squeeze through the miniature door, crying for a tiny, sunlit garden on the other side. Guillermo moved closer to her, pointing. 'See this guy? I saw him before, talking to her on the roof. He lives in that apartment.'

With startling clarity Guillermo was able to zoom in to a tall, thin man, his dark hair in a ponytail. He was standing in the front of the building, lighting a cigarette. Then he got into a small, dumpy white van and trundled off slowly.

'Think he's her captor?'

'Don't know.' Guillermo swiveled the lens again. 'I'm trying to get my bearings. See that big rectangle? That's east of here, that's the public market. So she's southwest from here. I'll drop you off at the hotel and go take a look.'

'No you're not,' said Laura, alarmed.

'I'm just going to look,' he said impatiently.

'What good is that going to do?'

'I don't know. We can't just do nothing. I took a picture of her more than a month ago, Laura. This is serious. Either I go check it out, or I call the police.'

'Do you even know where this building is? Looks like a maze out there.'

'I'll figure it out.'

Laura unzipped her backpack. 'Okay. You want to do this, let's do this properly. I'll go.'

'Why?'

'You have GPS on your phone, right? Hand it over.' She fiddled with it for a moment, then programmed her phone. 'Here. You can now track my phone on your GPS. I'm the red dot, you're the blue dot. Follow me using the camera obscura. Tell me if I'm going in the right direction. And watch the building, make sure that man doesn't come back. Call me if he does.' She fixed her Bluetooth earpiece on her ear.

'No, I'll go, you stay here.'

'Don't be so macho, for God's sake.' She was already leaving the room.

'Wait.' He disappeared down to the floor below. 'You'll need this.' He held out a bolt-cutter from one of the workmen's toolboxes.

She took it, jammed it in her backpack, and ran down the steps before he could say anything else.

*

Laura just had to get out of there. She couldn't be in that tower with Guillermo. He had leaned across her shoulder in that small room, and she had caught a whiff of his skin under his shirt. She knew they had slept together as teenagers, but suddenly that smell made her remember what it was like. It was not fair, she thought. You should not be able to smell someone else's skin in the dark. Those people who make perfume just didn't have a clue. Clean skin had a vocabulary of its own.

She plunged into the humid, gloomy afternoon. It was not yet the tourist season. The silent city now wore a cloud overhead like a thick frown.

He was married. That thin, handsome boy in the photos, in a shoebox in the garage – that boy had grown up and gone on, without her. Memories didn't grow up and get married. She was scandalized. Then again, she was always jealous and angry of anyone who was married, or who had kids. She had that option, once, but facing life with Stephen was so frightening that she turned him down when he proposed. She had a huge fall out with her parents and her sisters as a result. They really liked Stephen. They felt embarrassed and they couldn't go to the same church as his family after the breakup. She had to move from Sacramento to San Francisco to get away. Her friends decided that she must be lesbian. She allowed them to think that, because she was sick of being single. But now even gay people were getting married. Fuck them. The whole world was a marriage conspiracy. People pairing up; doors shutting.

47

For some reason Laura thought that Guillermo might have had the same life, that he would say, hello, I'm still single/I'm divorced, that's why I got back in touch with you. Of course someone like him would be comfortably nested by this age. His wife was probably beautiful. He probably had two small, photogenic children, about whom she would not ask.

She had thought that after Stephen, that she would very naturally find someone else. Just as she had thought that after Guillermo – but she was still in college then. There were so many guys. She was reasonably attractive; she had no trouble. She turned them around in her hands like pebbles at the beach, picking and discarding restlessly, looking for the right one. But what if?

Her earpiece buzzed. 'Laura? You're going the wrong way.'

She was thirty-five years old, single, an architect on a business trip, off to rescue some kid trapped in a house. Life could be worse. 'Well, which way should I go?'

'Do you see Calle San Jose? Try taking it straight down.'

San Jose, San Francisco, Sacramento. All these cities in California were now bewilderingly repeated in the streets of Cadiz. Her head was about to explode in a strange, inverted world. She looked at the GPS on her phone to orient herself. The street was deserted, save for a man standing outside a greengrocer's. He looked at her curiously. She returned to the plaza she had just left. She walked with her head down, purposefully, as if she knew what she was doing. A blue truck roared up the narrow street behind her. She ducked into a doorway, frightened. It cleared her by a few inches.

'I'm lost.'

'Just take that all the way, keep to that street and you'll be fine.'

She was now in a quiet neighborhood with balconies dripping with aloe vera and begonias. It looked decrepit. She passed by damp doorways opening into dim, blue-white courtyards of moldering marble and rusty wrought iron. There were no shops or people. Where the hell was everybody? Wasn't the siesta over? It began to rain.

'You're getting close.'

'It's raining.'

'I know. Hurry up, the light is fading.'

The streets formed an endless rabbit warren of cobblestones and faded façades. If she was in the mood, she would have stopped to look at every building that was being historically preserved, noted the names of the architecture firms on the billboards. She had studied building restoration, but ended up doing cafes, bars, and restaurants in San Francisco. That was all anybody ever wanted to pay for. She should have come here. Guillermo was in the right place. He had hit the mother lode of historical preservation, she thought enviously, passing a Roman amphitheater and following signs to the old city center.

Here, every window was shuttered. At times the buildings were so close together that the tops leaned over her broodingly. The fine drizzle scintillated down in the late afternoon light. She remembered a short story she read in college. Daphne du Maurier. About a couple (couples again!) and a mysterious blind woman. The husband followed a child through a twilit Venice. In the last, scary scene, the child turned around and unmasked himself as a crazed dwarf who stabbed him to death.

She turned a corner. Cadiz was a labyrinth of buildings of even height. She could not see any tall landmarks. The neighborhood looked tackier. She was outside a drab elementary school with mean-looking children lounging around. Little holes in the wall opened up into murky shops crammed with cheap toys and jars of pickles.

'Laura, stop,' said Guillermo urgently. 'It's right ahead. Look up.'

'The cream building with six windows?'

'That's it.'

She looked at the crumbly, eighteenth century façade with rusty white iron balcony railings. It looked like it was made of Stilton cheese. She couldn't see the roof terrace from the ground. Two young men appeared out of a doorway across the street. She thought they were looking at her, so she walked nonchalantly past them, pretending to have a phone conversation.

'Where are you going?'

'To see if there's a back entrance.'

'These townhouses are typically arranged around a central courtyard. See if the common front door is open. The back would probably be locked from the outside.'

She came to the front again and walked up confidently. The men watched her. She tried the main wooden door. To her surprise and relief, it swung inwards. She was in a tiny courtyard atrium crowded with potted plants, kids' tricycles, drying umbrellas. She smelled the acrid smell of frying peppers. She looked up. 'I'm in.'

'You are?'

'Yep. I'm going up. Keep a lookout for our guy.'

'Be careful.'

The interior of the building was whitewashed. The walls were paved with tiles painted in intricate blue and yellow designs. They were beautiful once. She walked up worn steps. She could hear someone's television playing and the yelping of a small dog somewhere. On the top floor she found a narrower staircase. It was protected by an iron gate with a small padlock. Looking around quickly, heart pounding, she clipped it with the bolt-cutter. That was easy. The one upstairs would be a bigger lock. She hoped she had enough strength.

She ran up the iron stairs and onto the roof terrace. The rain was now coming down in torrents. The puddles on the roof ate into her shoes right away. Out in the Atlantic, the storm was lavender-blue; the water near the beach remained the color of a robin's egg. Why did we think that a landscape looked like a Monet, when it was really the other way around, she thought. This was real. This was alive.

'Laura. The white van's coming back.'

Her neck tingled with fear. She hurried to the door and poised the bolt cutter on the shiny lock. Damn.

'Laura.'

'I'm trying to cut the lock!'

She squeezed with all her strength. The muscles on her chest twinged painfully. A curious, scrambling noise came from the inside.

Why didn't the girl say something? Was she mute?

What if there were more people inside?

What if there was a dwarf?

A leper?

What was on the other side of the door?

'Laura, get out of there! He's parked! He's coming out of the van!'

The lock snapped. She tugged it free and opened the door, but before she could see anything the woman was on top of her, hugging her and making soft, urgent little sounds.

'Go!' screamed Laura, shoving her down the steps.

They ran downstairs, tripping over umbrellas, shoes, potted plants – don't fall, don't fall! – then out through the front door. Laura dashed for the nearest alleyway, hoping it wasn't the one the man had parked in. Out of self-preservation she didn't even dare look back for the girl. She ducked into the first shop she saw. It was a tiny place selling Catholic statues and rosaries. The shopkeeper looked up from her newspaper, surprised.

'*Cuánto es?*' cried Laura, picking up a glittering rosary from the tray. Her hand was shaking. She rested it against the table so the shopkeeper wouldn't notice.

'*Diez.*'

Guillermo sounded frantic. 'Laura! Are you okay? Where are you?'

'Safe. In a church shop,' she hissed.

'He's gone into the building.'

'Where is she?'

'Long gone. I saw her running south, towards the highway.'

'Do you think he saw me?'

'No idea. Get out of there, come back to me.'

She liked the sound of that. 'Sorry, I can't hear you?'

'I said, hurry up and come back to me.'

Laura took the small package from the woman and went back out in the rain. Her heart was still pounding. At the end of the alley she found herself in a deserted pastel plaza with withered palms. She tore open the package and draped the rosary around herself. She wasn't religious, but its plastic cheer was comforting. She was crying silently with relief. She hoped he couldn't see her from where he was.

'Laura? You're crying.'

'I'm okay. I was so fucking scared.'

'Me too.'

'That was the craziest shit I ever did,' she said.

'Me too. Where do you think she will end up?'

'In a better place, hopefully.' She got up, looking around. 'I'm lost again.'

'It's easy from here. See that red building on one end of the plaza? Go towards it, turn left, make the first right, then walk up Calle del Sacramento all the way.'

Wiping her nose with the sleeve of her sweater, Laura put away her GPS phone. She didn't need it anymore. There was a resolute clarity in Guillermo's directions.

There was the red building. Left, right. Calle del Sacramento. She recognized the tower in the distance.

'I see you,' said Guillermo. 'I'm coming down.'

Relieved, Laura pulled up her collar against the rain and broke into a run.

The flying bush cow helmet mask

Jenny Newman

A man laughed in the dark beyond our window, so long and loud that Frik's old yard dog barked. Frik jumped, and so would you if just two years ago armed men had raided your farm while you slept, stolen your possessions and turned your animals on to the road.

The man laughed again. Our mattress dipped and grumbled. Frik was sitting up to check the bush cow mask was safe.

He kept it on a shelf above our bed: the only thing of value left him by the thieves, who'd probably felt afraid of its power. Knobbly wooden horns sprang out of its brow and its tapering muzzle gleamed in the strip of light from the hall. Long ago, Frik had told me, the mask used to 'fly': tribal women wore it like a helmet when soaring above the Karoo in search of their ancestors' graves. I was glad that, though he'd spent his government compensation, he refused to sell it to a bank or a museum. Though I knew its eyes were only holes in the red clay of its face, I liked to believe it watched over our bed as we slept or lay awake, like now, side by side in the Johannesburg night.

My hand reached for the rucksack Frik made me keep beneath the bed in case we needed to run for it during the night. It bulged with emergency clothes, a roll of rand notes and a lump of potter's clay. In his, Frik had stowed an aerial photo of his farm, a credit card and a Glock wrapped in a pair of shorts.

People were starting to chat over the thump of a drum. My pulse rate slowed: just squatters on a neighbouring veranda. Their stereo blared. My foot beat time as if turning my potter's wheel. In the Karoo, when sleepless, I used to wander into my garden, smoke a cigarette and watch for shooting stars. But Frik's house was alarmed and the least movement beyond it summoned a guard from Secur-It DogMan, siren blaring and blue light flashing on his Ranger roof.

Frik sighed.

I stroked his chest.

I was letting my fingers slither inside his boxers when he started to snore, a regular puffing sound. Though my hand roamed over his cushiony belly, his prick stayed sulkily small against the soft skin of his thighs. I'd have liked to switch on the light and ask, not why he'd been unfaithful, just why we'd stopped having sex. But he'd have put on his hangdog face and muttered about feeling stressed, making me sorry for him instead of myself, as I'd have liked, who'd followed him to a place nobody wanted to live in any more.

So I lay breathing his smells of sweat and Van der Hum mixed with the scent of *dagga* drifting through the bars while the bush cow seemed to nod in time to the pulsing drum.

Ntombi was born on Frik's farm and her name meant Little Girl: a name she'd clearly outgrown with her breasts and burly hips and the violent swipes of her broom at the parquet round my feet. She stopped as I crossed the hall, gave me a knowing smile and glanced at our bedroom door. Surely she hadn't spied me repacking my rucksack?

She watched me as I walked to the veranda where Frik was downing his second pot of coffee. Wisteria scrambled up the gable at his back and twined itself around the security sign. A silhouette against its triangle of white, Secur-It DogMan stood, prick-eared, angling his snout at the sky, his hind legs balanced on the logo: *Shoot To Kill*. When you came in from the street and unlocked the front door, you'd twenty-two seconds to key in your special code. Only the week before, I'd muddled up the digits and the guard had arrived, pointing his gun and yelling at me to lie flat. If Frik hadn't appeared and reeled off the proper numbers I might have been shot dead.

'I'm changing the code,' he said in a voice so low it was almost lost in the roar of an overhead plane. Ntombi's made

too many pals among the locals. This one will be known by
only you and me, so choose one you won't forget.

'28011950! The day my mother was born.'

He frowned as if my feckless genes might sabotage his
system. My mother had been irresponsible, he'd said the other
day, letting herself get pregnant by a Coloured man – and just
an odd job man, at that.

The street bell rang. Frik walked down the garden path,
looked through the spy-hole and unlocked the door. Caiaphas
was waiting on the pavement, wearing his faded army shirt
with odd-sized pink and red buttons. Frik's dog bared her
teeth at him and snarled.

'Get in the car, Caiaphas,' said Frik. 'The madam's on
her way.' He kissed my cheek. 'Have you got your cell phone?'

I patted my jeans pocket.

'Give my love to *ou sis,'* he called as I climbed in the
back of the cab.

Caiaphas eased us through the crowds on our street,
men and women, old and young, skin treacle-brown or yellow
or terra-cotta or purple-black like plums. All colours except
white. Most of the houses were formerly grand, with high
Dutch gables. Knobs of broken stucco lay scattered across
their lawns and men in shorts and vests lolled on their *stoeps.* In
the sun baking the pavements on either side, traders had set up
stalls heaped with over-ripe avocados and fly-infested water
melon slices. In front of the trestles more traders squatted,
threading beads on wire or guarding rows of soapstone
warriors. Children squashed their noses against the car
window, trying to sell me grubby sweets made from tinned
pineapple chunks. At the bus stop for the airport, a queue of
people jostled in the sun, surrounded by so many boxes and
possessions wrapped in blankets you might have thought they
were fleeing from a war zone.

The air struck cold as I wove across the café where Ilse
was already sipping her Iced Muggachino. Though Frik had
grown soft and stooped, his sister had kept her square,
stockwoman's figure as if she still spent her days on horseback
herding cattle, not working part-time as a teller in a bank.

55

I pulled up a chair and mopped my face with my sleeve. Ilse never sweated and would have preferred a table out in the sun, fending off hawkers and commenting on the passers-by.

'How's little brother?' As always, she sounded concerned: poor Frikkie had failed to adapt to city life.

'He's drinking too much,' I said. 'A bottle of wine every night, sometimes two, then several *dops* before bed.'

Ilse raised her almost invisible eyebrows. No one outside the family censured Frikkie.

'And during the day,' I continued, 'he does nothing but sit and watch sport.'

Ilse gave that picture a flick of her mental *sjambok*.

'You should get a job. Then you wouldn't fret about what he does or doesn't do.'

I imagined myself on the kerb outside our house, selling what Frik had taken to calling my wonky pots.

'It's hard, sharing a kiln with thirty or forty people.'

'I meant a proper job. Something that gets you out of the house.'

'Frik says all the arty jobs are going to the Blacks.'

Ilse gave me her thin, bleached stare. 'With a bit of a push you could pass for black yourself.'

I waved away the waiter bringing my coffee. 'Time for my haircut, I lied.'

Ilse twitched at the cardigan draped over her bony shoulders.

My cheeks still hot, I stalked to the other end of the mall where *First 4 Hair* fitted me in straightaway. The junior spent ten minutes massaging my scalp. It was Frik who'd begged me to come with him – told me they'd found him a little house in Jo'burg – that Ntombi would actually like me to throw my pots in her *kaya*.

My muscles relaxed. I let the junior file and paint my nails while Marlene straightened my hair and talked about local rapes.

'Life's no better than under apartheid,' she said, 'except now it's the *tsotsis* who keep you indoors.'

Crinkly curls sprawled on the salon floor and my face in the mirror looked smug under my neat new fringe. Frik would approve of the style and of my shell-pink nails, and be pleased

I'd phoned Caiaphas and asked him to take me home instead of trusting any old driver from the rank.

Frik was standing in the garden, his face in anxious folds. He shoved his cell phone in his pocket as I hurried up the path.

'The mask has gone,' he said. 'It was Ntombi who noticed when she was cleaning our room.'

'Have you phoned the police?'

'Yes, and they were useless. Said crime's so out of hand they've got no time to spare. What's worse, the bloody insurance won't pay up because there's not the slightest trace of anyone breaking in.'

'So what are you going to do?'

'Ntombi says we should call in a sangoma.'

I caught sight of the maid hovering just inside the house, smiling her knowing smile.

'Go to your *kaya*,' I said. 'I'm talking to the *baas*.'

She huffed across the hall and slammed the back door behind her.

'You shouldn't be so rude to her,' said Frik. 'She knows the man who throws the bones for Bafana Bafana and makes a *muti* for Garage Jax whenever they launch a CD.'

'Then it's stupid to get involved. With these primitive things you can soon get out of your depth.'

'You've missed the point. Ntombi's pretty clever.'

'I know how clever she is.'

Frik's eyes scurried uncertainly over my face. 'She thinks the thief is almost certainly local and that a powerful elder might persuade him to give back the mask.'

'Then do what you like,' I said.

The sangoma arrived next day, a compact, bespectacled man I'd sometimes noticed chatting to Ntombi at our gate. Instead of tribal dress, he wore a cream linen suit and smelt strongly of Paco Rabanne. Nor did he throw the bones or produce an evil-smelling *muti*, just asked Ntombi for a tin of Lion Ale which he dribbled on to the floor in the corners of every room, arm outstretched so as not to splash his loafers. Frik and I brought up the rear, following Ntombi who swabbed at the puddles and tutted at the stains. When he reached our bedroom the sangoma stood on tiptoe and ran his hands over the empty shelf.

'Your maid is right,' he said, turning to face us. 'The mask is still close by – though who knows for how long?'

He held out a plump, pink palm. Frik counted out one hundred rand in notes. The sangoma cupped his hands and bowed to show the payment was generous.

'Someone has borrowed your cow for a purpose. A sacred purpose, I think. Maybe your bush cow wants to take to the air.'

That night, I dreamt that the mask had returned to its place on the shelf and its knobbly horns were swaying in time to the ceiling fan. I lifted it down, slid it over my head and looked through its eye-holes at Frik as he slept through the reddening dawn. I launched myself out of the window and over the razor-wire on the fence around our yard. The grid of the sleeping city widened below me, its pinpricks of light racing along its runways, and mine dumps rising like pyramids round its edge. As I coasted over the cooked earth of the south, the cracks in its surface glowed like marks on an ancient pot.

Frik woke me early because he'd decided to throw a party – to cheer himself up, he said.

That morning, he sounded more cheerful than ever before, ordering ostrich steaks and seafood over the phone, telling the garden boy how to erect the awning and laughing with Ntombi by the stove. Bang, bang, bang, went their knives on the chopping board as they hacked mealies into chunks for roasting on the *braai*. The house filled with the smell of charred flesh mixed with lighter fuel while stringy women in floral dresses flocked into the yard followed by men in polo shirts over bionic chests. The sangoma slipped through a side door, the only Black among the leathery, sun-tanned guests. He helped himself to ale while Simon stoked the *braai* and Ntombi served the women with glasses of Nederburg. I was checking my haircut in front of the bedroom mirror when I noticed Frik's bulk filling the doorway behind me.

'Aren't you coming to talk to our guests?'

'I'll be there in a minute or two.'

He shambled across the hall and was met by a surge of laughter. I closed the door and dropped to my knees by the bed. I hadn't even bothered to close my rucksack, so my fingertips soon located the sturdy horns, the holes of the eyes and glossily rounded nose. I swung the pack on to my back and slid the mask over my head. Through its eyeholes the room looked cluttered yet faraway. Breathing a smell of sweat mixed with coconut oil, I squinted at the bed where I'd so often lain awake and where, the day before yesterday, coming home early, I'd found Frik and Ntombi sitting side by side.

I paused in the empty hall: still time to gulp a lungful of air and restore the mask to its shelf. Its clay grew warm as it settled its weight on my shoulders. On reaching the veranda, I took a last look at the yard: life takes unpredicted shapes as the wheel gathers speed, and the hardest part of loving is forsaking, whether you're leaving your tribe or leaving your man.

Ilse stared at me from the lawn at the foot of the steps.

'Is that you? Where did you find the mask?'

I dodged past her and on to the path.

'Take it off,' she called. 'It's a valuable family heirloom and it doesn't belong to you.'

I lowered my horns. A bellicose moo ripped out of my bush cow mouth. Silence fell on the husbands turning steaks on the *braai,* on their wives gossiping under the awning, and even on the dog yapping at the sangoma.

'Speak to her, Frik,' yelled Ilse, tapping a number into her cell phone.

But Frik stood in silence between Ntombi and the Sangoma.

'Goodbye, Frikkie,' I said.

Half-cloaked by smoke from the fire, he lifted a hand. Somewhere, streets away, a siren rang.

'Hurry, Bush Cow,' called the sangoma. 'Your time has come to fly.'

My feet started to dance. The garden swayed and tilted. I danced past the men's meaty faces and the women's questioning stares. I danced through the door and on to the street past piles of avocados and water melon slices and soapstone statuettes. Secur-It DogMan car was manoeuvring through the stalls, siren wailing and cold blue eye winking on its roof, but nobody cleared a path for it or pointed in my direction, not even the children selling sweets on the kerb. And nobody tried to block me as I danced towards the stop, pushed to the top of the queue and hopped on the airport bus.

Three Shells

Zoë Teale

Because there were three people in Motohiro's life that he wished were still with him, he decided that he would make three shells in their memory. He would bury them close to the sea, on a beach somewhere remote, somewhere that there would not be people forever passing and searching. Somewhere beautiful and empty, where the shells would sit undisturbed for some time. They would be found, of course. One day a visitor would see a glitter of sunlight that was too bright for the place, or feel something metallic amongst the wet pebbles. Maybe a child would find one, searching rock pools for a furled anemone. Or a young man looking for St Columba's green marble, having breathed the simple life on the Saint's Island. Maybe they would be grubbed by the landscape then, and not spotted as gold. Or else they might be shinier for their sea-polish. He would not know.

The English lady had given him the idea. She had said as she stood embarrassed, cupping a tiny bowl, 'It seems as though you could find one on a beach and feel it belonged there, as though it were a shell.' He had liked the way she spoke, and felt uneasy about what he had made.

The worth of the gold was not much to him. He did not want for much, and he had easy access to the material. He was tiring of his bowls, although they had bought him fame; their curved patterns no longer looked as natural to him as once they had, for too many people had photographed them, too many well-dressed women and men in city suits had introduced themselves as great admirers of his work. He was finishing a commission for such a gentleman, a delicate bowl with beaten hearts barely visible, a Valentine's present, not for the English lady, his wife, but for a younger woman whom the man was thinking of ending his marriage of many years for. Motohiro's silence encouraged such confession. So often clients spat out their world to him, and he nodded, remained composed, made them something beautiful to go along with.

The English lady had said, 'Imagine finding a golden leaf on a tree, or a golden rock sitting among other rocks at the side of a lake? Maybe it would make people look at things more.' Her husband seemed to stare straight through her, Motohiro thought.

Once he had wanted to make people look more closely at things. But recently he had lost sight of why he was making.

How empty the bowl seemed, how hollow it rung as he beat it. He wanted something different. He would make a shell for his mother and for his father, and one for his father's father who was the only one of his grandparents that he had known. His grandfather had been a potter, and Motohiro when small would sit in his studio in Hokkaido, looking out at the snow, the fire of the kiln keeping the workplace warm. While his friends called and rolled and made sculptures from the snow and ice, he worked at models with clay. Mostly he made animals, simple animals; cats, for he loved the smooth curved back of the sleeping cat, and the way that it tucked its tail in neatly, forming a circle.

His parents had been teachers; his father taught Art in the High School, finding that there was no demand for his own paintings on the most northerly island of Japan; his mother worked with Ainu children, and was always seen as odd for this reason. All four were outsiders in their way. And he was, still, despite his success. His customers were not those he was born among. No one in Japan bought his work. He had chosen to live in a city, in a continent that was not his own.

As Motohiro beat the gold, he thought again of the English woman, and felt saddened by his part in her story.

The man had come by to query something and had left her in the car, like a dog, staring from the back seat. She sat patiently. Motohiro watched her, not listening to the man talk on about his new happiness. He watched as finally, wondering where her husband had got to, she opened the car door. Her face was lined but not tired at all, as though she still despite her age had a long way to go, as a stone appears old yet timeless. The three of them had stood uncomfortably in the hall, the husband flushed and Motohiro pale with the sudden recognition of what he was doing. 'What do you do?' she had asked. And Motohiro had put one of his miniature bowls in her hand. 'Malcolm is such a supporter of the arts', she had said over her shoulder as her husband guided her out into the cold London morning.

He hardly wanted to give the bowl over. He felt that he ought to say something, but he did not know what he could say and it was not his way to say much. He had never fought anyone, never even raised his voice. He had never judged anyone until now. But he did not feel right about his making of a beautiful thing which would play its part in the wooing of a new woman and the destruction of a long union. As he worked the bowl, beating the gold against the wooden cups; as he carved a wooden hammer to make the beaten heart patterning, and beat the gold again with this, the wooden heart, he thought of the woman's face. He wished that he was making the bowl for her. He made a life for her. He wondered if she had ever had children, or if she had yearned for them, felt empty without them, turned in on herself. Her face was not that of the other rich wives that he met. Her voice was not false, as some seemed to him. She pictured his gold tossed by the sea sometime in the future of the world, returning to its natural place. Her presence, her face, a few clear words, had given him ideas for a different kind of work.

He no longer found any pleasure in the feel of the bowl. The ridges between the beaten planes caught at the light, each subtle heart edged with spark. It was rough and beautiful, but to Motohiro it no longer had what he was looking for, the beauty of the uncut jewel, the beauty of the natural. Nothing to him that was made by man could approach what was truly lovely. Nothing that was dishonest or contrived. Perhaps this was the reason his patron's wife returned to his thoughts. For in that moment, when he had seen her searching through the glass of the car window as they drove away, she had appeared to him as absolutely beautiful as a human could be. Simple. The clean cut grey wool dress, the old blue eyes.

He wondered what he would be remembered for. The image of small objects scattered about the earth, symbolising those who had been, appealed to him. He had never been vain. He had never felt a desperate need to be remembered for anything.

He would make an oyster, a small one, for his grandfather, and for his father a clam, and his mother a curled snail shell, of the type that she had collected sometimes on walks by the sea, making jewellery with the Ainu children from them. These three would be monuments. They would be his equivalent of a memorial statue. Wherever they ended up that is what they would be. He went to the seaside at Dungeness on a rainy day, looked at the simple gardens with their fences of smoothed drift-wood, their paths of pebbles, now multiplying at the foot of the nuclear plant. He gathered shells on the shore, to make moulds, and returned to London in the dark, feeling the water under his shoes as he walked to his front door, for at times when it rained and the rain had nowhere to run it felt as though the city was sinking. As he turned the light on in his studio, the yet uncollected heart bowl glinted.

Once begun he could not stop. Often he worked like this, whether for himself or others. But now he worked more furiously than ever, through the night, casting the shells and choosing the most perfect to be turned to gold. When the telephone rang in the morning and he answered it, he could not tell who spoke, but he heard himself saying that it was not quite complete, that in a day or two, no more, it could be collected.

Somewhere far back he remembered that his grandfather had made a tea bowl for an old samurai. The bowl had looked like mud. But it was hard, for holding the bright green tea of the tea ceremony. Motohiro had knelt, listening to his grandfather and the old man discussing the bowl, muttering in low voices, expressing their pleasure with a clicking sound that came from deep in their throats, their eyes crinkled, like two ancient reptilian creatures raising their heads against the earth. When the telephone rang again, he did not answer.

On Valentine's day, Motohiro left the house early. He took a black cab to an address in the west of the city, and rang the doorbell. The English lady, the wife, was in a dark grey woollen gown, and her hair was untidy. She smiled as he handed her the package, which was wrapped roughly in paper and string. 'These are for you', Motohiro said, 'The letter inside will explain.'

He took the train to Inverness. He had never been there, and the name reminded him of Dungeness, but when he arrived it was not what he was looking for. He wanted to go on, as his grandfather's family had once gone on North until they had reached the winter snows of Hokkaido. He took another train, and a boat, and the next day he was in the Orkney Islands. On a wide sand beach with not a cottage in sight, he dug deep, until his hole was filled with over a foot of water. Trying to stop the sand from folding back in on itself, he undid his own parcel, ran his fingers across the hundreds of beaten hearts, and buried the bowl under the water and the sand. When it was gone he did not really know why he had done it. Perhaps it was a stupid thing to do. But it was done.

*

The woman read the letter carefully. She held the three shells in her palm and felt them grow warm as she read:

These three I would like buried, perhaps on a beach somewhere – wherever you wish to take them. For me, it is better not to know where they are, but just to know they are there somewhere, on a sort of journey.

Once, before marriage, before London, she had been in the Outer Hebrides. On the island of Barra, she had been rowed to a castle in the harbour by a young man. She had spent a day with him on that fortified rock. There had been no other visitors, but in the late afternoon a seal had come and watched them with its cat-like face on one side, whiskers quivering. The man had said then that she must come to live there. And she had laughed it off.

For the first time, through many years, she could hear her laugh again, and it sounded horrible to her now. She began to think about things that she had kept buried for a very long time. When her husband telephoned to say that he would be late again, she took the map and laid it on the dining room table, tracing the coast until it grew dark. Two days after Motohiro had left his golden shells, she was heading away from her own house, quietly, small bag in hand. She took a train to the airport, flew to Glasgow, and then onward in a tiny twin-otter plane to the beach at the north of Barra, where she landed at low tide. The sand was full of the shapes that the sandworms left, tiny sculptures that the next tide would flatten. One of the men working in the airport gave her a lift to the south of the island.

Dusk was falling across the bay, and the sky was becoming a bruised purple in colour. The castle stood tiny and black against it.

She stepped onto the wooden jetty, walking out over the water. Two of the shells she dropped, one up close to the harbour wall, one a little further from the edge. The last she threw far out toward the castle, watching it arc through the darkening sky before falling. Each made a gentle suck as they disappeared, something like a small mammal feeding. The sea was flat as a mirror and the ripples made neat circles out and out and then were gone.

*

Motohiro slept well. In the morning the high skies of Orkney made him feel that the world had grown taller. Past the middle of February, and spring would be coming. He thought he would stay, and see it come here. Something of those he had loved had visited him, and would be with him in an altered way from now on. He watched an oyster-catcher picking its way across the sand, legs like twigs and beak like a long blade. He felt in his pocket for his mobile phone, and turned it off without looking down.

The Visit

Karen Stevens

It's my own fault,' my father informs me when I enter his conservatory. 'Self-inflicted.' He looks morose, a little drunk. His left arm is held against his chest in a blue rubber sling, his left eye is cut and swollen, the bruising as brown and purple as liver.

I kiss his cheek and catch a waft of beer. A pint of home-made brew is set up on a side table next to his wicker chair, where his right hand can easily reach it. The top is like the frothing scum that lines the sea at the shore. I sit on the chair opposite, avoiding the tiny sofa where Maureen will no doubt sit.

'How you feeling?' I ask.

'I'm not happy; not happy.'

It is November, yet there are still vivid spots of red begonia flowers and dots of yellow winter jasmine amongst the brown stumps of plants. The paint on the metal shed peels away in green curls and strips, a small sign that they are not quite keeping on top of everything.

In the kitchen Maureen is frantically making tea. Cups chink. Things bang against the draining board in her mad effort to ensure we are not left to talk alone for too long. For twenty-nine years she has successfully wedged herself between my father and me; always the one to answer the phone; always the one to answer the door. Once, in earlier days, I rang to say I'd be over some time between two and five, and then didn't turn up. It was satisfying knowing I'd made her a prisoner in this house for the day, constantly looking out for me through the front window.

My father coughs.

'See the garden's all set for winter, then,' I say.

'The garden's *not* set up. We've only managed to dig

the first load of manure into half the vegetable garden. Maureen's had to put a stop to the other load that was meant to be arriving tomorrow.'

My father looks down at his left arm uselessly. His good arm shakes as he raises his tankard to his lips. The room grows still around us as we both concentrate on him drinking beer, the yeasty air thick with the ache that is always between us. Into the silence of the conservatory comes the image I'd had in my dream last night, of Frank lying naked on our bed, stretched out like a pale starfish.

'Well!' Maureen puffs, as if exhausted. Her '*Well!*' – brittle and sharp as cheese wire – is designed to cut through conversation. 'I don't suppose *you* want tea if you're drinking,' she berates my father.

Since his accident, Maureen told me hurriedly – dramatically – on the doorstep, he will not stop drinking. He starts at twelve and goes on until he passes out.

'Has he told you what happened?' Maureen hands me my tea, and I feel a little ashamed before saying, 'No. No he hasn't.'

'Now, we didn't call you when he was taken into hospital because there was nothing you could have done. We would have just worried you unnecessarily.'

I am, as usual, an afterthought. It is their duty to inform me of my father's accident at some point, and my duty to visit at some point. It is better not to visit. In the months between, all my striving to put something good in the place of hurt is always destroyed with a single visit. Maureen sits on the sofa and looks to my father for back-up when she sees my face tighten.

'Besides, it was my own fault,' my father adds. 'I'd had too much to drink and fell off the kerb into the road … between The Yew Tree and The Maypole… '

His chin shivers. I don't want to see it. Outside, sparrows squabble on the bird table.

'And when I tried to get out of the road and back on the pavement I tripped up the kerb. And that's about the last I remember.'

A crack runs through the centre of my father's voice.

He looks at Maureen in a helpless, childish way, and tears swell. Maureen turns to look at me in the same helpless way. *See,* her eyes accuse. *See what you've done to him.* 'Hard as stone,' that's what she once called me.

Maureen's head has shrunk onto her shoulders and looks as if it will fall inside her body at any moment. It is almost pleasing to see her body softening and caving in with old age. In my school years she was all angles and nasty edges. She'd never met my mother but gave the impression of knowing her so intimately, that she would often fall into lengthy rants about things like the *obscene* number of nighties my mother had apparently owned. It gave me strange dreams; it made me dread coming home from school.

I see Frank stretched out on our bed, his skin the colour of egg whites in the square of moonlight from our bedroom window. In my dream I'd reached out and smoothed the top of his black hair, nervously at first. And when he didn't stir I grew braver, opening my fingers to let his thick hair slide between them. *Frank,* I'd whispered, *do you like me?*

Maureen is telling me more about the accident that put my father in hospital for two days. When he arrived the nurses gave him something to sedate him, then something stronger, then a shot of morphine for pain relief; then another shot, but nothing worked. He kept ripping his sling off and the heart monitor attached in sticky pads to his chest; the nurses couldn't prevent him from constantly getting off the bed. 'You'd think at seventy he'd be easy to calm. Even the nurses were shocked!' Maureen finishes, her voice trembling at the thought of the life force that must still exist somewhere deep inside my inebriated father.

'You see the documentaries of people being abusive and I'm ashamed to say I was like that, wasn't I, love; swearing and threatening the poor nurses.' My father tries to say something more, but the words are lodged like rocks in his throat.

'He kept asking if the dogs were alright in the rain!' Maureen laughs, making light of my father's dismay. 'Anyway, we know you're not like that normally, don't we?' Maureen nods her head at me, urging me to agree.

The phone rings. Alarm bells flash in Maureen's eyes.

'That'll be Jean.' She heaves herself up. 'I won't be long,' she warns.

My father drinks beer and stares out at his precious garden. At the far end CDs strung on lengths of twine flash silver in the wind to prevent the pigeons from eating his Brussels sprouts. Once, when I was a child, I'd watched my father walking along his neat rows of vegetables, turning leaves over gently to check for greenfly. He picked a tomato and studied it carefully, then brought it up to his lips and kissed it.

Frank, I'd whispered, *do you like me?*

Angie was a friend until she'd visited in those shoes. She pretended she'd worn them for my benefit, but we all knew she wanted Frank to see her in them. 'There's another pair that would suit you,' she'd told me, 'something to perk you up a bit.' And the guilt of being trapped inside this empty, thin, sexless skin as Angie paraded around our living room, twisting her slim ankles from left to right for Frank to inspect the quality of the Italian leather.

'I'd best get back soon,' I say, looking at the brown skin of my cooling tea.

'When I woke up in the hospital, it gave me a turn, it did.' My father's drunken tongue trips over the words as he tries to get them out before Maureen returns. 'I'd fallen off the curb at the exact same spot as your mother's accident.'

My stomach falls at the mention of my mother.

'Ask me anything about the accident,' my father says quickly.

My cheeks burn with embarrassment; we have never spoken about my mother.

'I'm seventy now. Soon it'll all be buried with me. Ask me anything,' he insists.

I was five when my mother was knocked off her bike by a car, yet I have no memory of her. Occasionally, when I was a child and the accident was still real and raw, a relative used to say something – *she was a sun-worshipper; she loved a good dance; remember that time when* – and my father would halt the conversation with a clipped response. It felt as if the relative was unwrapping a present and my father was quickly wrapping it up again. I hated him for it.

My father turns away from his garden and looks at me

with his battered eye. In all my knowing life he has never really looked at me. He looks just to the left or just to the right. Or else his eyes search out the safety of Maureen's.

I think of our past together – always lived functionally, as if I was a burden, a duty he could hardly stomach - and the worst time (was it the worst?) when I'd stood at the edge of the vegetable garden, waiting. He was digging, the edges of him crisped pink with the sun. He knew I was there, hovering like a ghost on the path, but chose to dig harder, his back juddering as he thrust his spade into the mud, refusing to look at me; refusing to give me even the chance to ask for pocket money.

In my dream Frank's hand was as cold as metal when I'd lifted it from our bed and put it on my breast. He'd kept it there, unmoving, not rubbing or stroking, just there, as if it was a punishment.

'I'm seventy now. It'll all be buried with me,' my father says. His eyes are pleading, brimming with unhappiness, as if he wants something from me that I cannot and will not give. Not now. This desperate look, as sharp as fish flashing through water, is a look I sometimes catch before Maureen wades in and talks it back into the depths.

Maureen arrives, flummoxed. She puts her hands to her head when she sees my father's face.

'Frank's left me,' I say to the conservatory, but Maureen is flapping around my father: flapping, flapping, flapping. Finally, Frank left me for Angie. I could have pulled him back with just a touch or a word – a simple word. *Hard as stone* as I walked away and into our garden, the silky plumes of pampas grass trembling against the sky.

Saved

Jane Rogers

When Alice lifted a corner of the tarpaulin, a cidery whiff of rotting apples escaped. Leaning closer in the failing light she saw that the trailer was full of them. Excellent. Had she not clearly explained to Head that she needed the trailer to move her Grandma's bed?

'I haven't had time to get rid of them,' he told her.

'Don't you want them?'

'Couldn't sell 'em. There's a glut.' He was called Head because he was always off it, according to her brother Nick: Nick who was skulking in Oxford like the idle toad he was, pretending his term hadn't finished yet.

'They would have kept better if you hadn't left them in plastic bags.' She glanced around his so-called garden which was piled with rusty old bits of farm equipment and random builders' supplies, and saw there was nowhere to put them.

'Dump 'em. Take 'em to the tip.' He turned towards his peeling front door. 'I need the trailer Sunday, OK?'

Quite a few of the apples in the first bag were alright, as far as she could see. A bit wormy, and the odd brown patch, but plenty of them could be saved. How could he throw away perfectly good food? 'Trash the planet why don't you?' she muttered to his closing door. She backed up the car and attached the trailer to the rear bumper, winding the rope around both ends so the weight was evenly distributed. It would be fine over a short journey. If her parents had had a better car it would have had a tow bar. Well, if they'd had a better *bigger* car, there would've been room in it for the bed.

She turned cautiously out of his gateway and eased the car up through the gears, watching the trailer in her mirror. It was fine until she pulled out onto the main road. There she got stuck behind a car which had tinsel wound round its aerial and a diamond shaped sign dangling in its back window, bearing the legend *Fab Mum on Board!* The Fab Mum stopped at every junction, major and minor, and allowed all the traffic waiting there to file out in front of her. Each time Alice had to stop, no matter how gently, the trailer jolted the car. By the time she got home her teeth were on edge.

She began to unload the bags of apples into the hall. They were heavy so it wasn't safe to use the handles; she clutched the plastic bags to her chest and realised, too late, that festering juice was smearing all over her leather jacket. The bags pretty much blocked the hall. She might as well sort them immediately for the full joyful Friday night experience. Danny would probably be getting ready to go out partying, hunting for some new female. Well hey, why should Alice care? This was so much more fun. Close inspection revealed that each bag contained soft brown putrefying apples mixed in with the green. Swiftly she filled the kitchen bin with rotten apples and the washing up bowl and clothes-basket with half-bad ones. It was strange the way they went; you'd pick one up that was green but then its underside was brown, with a kind of raised dottiness where the two colours met. When you cut it in two, the decay inside went right up the core to the top. All you could save was the top sliver of the apple's cheeks. She imagined slicing Danny out of her system like this, like a surgeon removing a tumour. Even the white, fresh-looking slices still seemed to have an aftertaste of rot. She sprinkled them lavishly with cinnamon and cloves. Then her mother came home from hospital visiting and picked up an apple with a half-dead wasp attached.

Once things had quietened down, they took a bottle of red into the sitting room, where the box of Christmas decorations sat accusingly on the sofa.

'If I'd known you'd have to go to all this trouble –' her mother said.

The wine at home wasn't as sour as the wine Danny chose in York. 'When are you getting the tree? Did you tell Dad why I couldn't visit?'

'I haven't got time to get a tree! All he talks about is Grandma's. I could understand it if he'd been there even once.'

Grandma had died in the spring leaving her house full of dirty old junk to Dad. Now suddenly there was a buyer who wanted to move in before Christmas. Alice watched her mother drinking. Her face was puffy, she seemed to have aged disproportionately since Alice started university.

'He's alright, Dad? I mean a hip replacement's routine, isn't it?'

'Yep. They'll get him up on his feet tomorrow, the nurse told me. Two to three days and I'll have him on my hands here needing waiting on.'

'I'll visit tomorrow after I've moved the bed.'

'He wants me to go and look through Grandma's stuff – I'm at the library till 5 tomorrow, I've told him –'

'Mum there's no point.'

'Her knick knacks, her photos, he says there are things of sentimental –'

'No there aren't. And where would you put them anyway? This house is completely stuffed.' Alice's university possessions were heaped in a pathetic mound on the landing, since her mother had filled Alice's room with a rowing machine and bags of remnants to make a quilt.

'Alice, I don't see why the clearance people can't drop the bed off.'

'The man told me he'd need another van for the bed. Look, you want it don't you? I'm happy to fetch it.'

'I don't want it. It's your father who wants it. He claims its some kind of antique.'

'Well I'm not saving it if you're not going to use it, Mum.'

'Oh we'll use it! It's not as if our bed's anything to write home about.'

'OK then.'

'I can't understand why Nick's not back for Christmas. He could have given you a hand.'

'Mum, I can manage –'

'The whole thing's ridiculous. We'll end up paying the clearance people more than the stuff is worth.' Her mother took a bottle from the sideboard, poured a mouthful into her wine glass and swirled it round, then drained the pink results. 'Would you like some whisky?' she said, pouring it into the rinsed glass. 'Sorry, I can't be bothered with getting more glasses.'

You come home from university with issues – real issues: like deciding to drop out of your course, and splitting up with Danny, and having paid six months rent in advance when now you can't go on living in the same house as him: you come home and your parents have turned into an alcoholic and an invalid, and *you* have to help *them*.

It would be all right. She would be helpful now, and tell them about leaving York after Christmas. It would soften the blow. She took a sip of the fiery whisky. 'What's your badge, Mum?'

'Oh – it's supposed to be an angel, I think. You press it and it flashes –' She demonstrated. 'They were giving them out at work.'

'Cool! Can I see?'

Her mother passed her the little pink and white plastic angel, the tips of her wings were flashing yellow. Alice laughed.

'Keep it if you like,' her mother said. 'They've got all sorts. I'll bring you a reindeer to go with it.' Alice pinned the angel to her jumper. 'Come here and give us a hug,' said her mother, smiling at last. 'It's good to have you home.'

By midnight her mother, sedated with Famous Grouse, had gone to bed, and Alice had filled another bin liner with peel, core and bad bits. Danny had not texted her. Four saucepans of apples were stewing on the four cooker rings and the air was thick with steam. Various forms of wildlife - spiders, slugs and maggoty things - had been revived enough by the warmth to start crawling up the walls. Excellent, she had saved a whole eco-system. Alice turned everything off and went to bed, hoping Danny was so drunk that he would suffer humiliating erectile dysfunction. Assuming he was with someone else. Which she might as well assume.

She was awake at six so she got up and dealt with the rest of the apples. Then she sat on the doorstep to have her breakfast cigarette, and worried about money. Maybe she should offer to clear Grandma's whole house and sell the stuff on eBay. But it'd have to go into storage and that would cost. The clearance people were charging the earth for storage. She should go online and check prices. All of it was rubbish but things like the Formica kitchen table and red plastic chairs, they were probably retro by now, probably collectors' items.

The post came; a card from Nick in Oxford. It showed two shrunken heads from the Pitt Rivers Museum, against a queasy green and yellow background. On the back he had scrawled, *Pater and Mater, Yo! Giving Xmas a miss this year END CAPITALISM NOW! X*

Excellent.

Her mother was getting ready for work and fussing about the apples. She didn't have enough freezer boxes for them. She didn't want Alice to put the rotten ones in the compost. 'It'll be full, I won't be able to use it all winter.'

Alice explained patiently that it would be full of decaying vegetable matter, which is what compost bins are for. But her mother was surprisingly assertive. Alice ended up reloading bags of slimy remains into the trailer and scratching herself on its sharp tailgate. The pain was a welcome distraction from the larger pain of the world's idiocy. She drove carefully through the suburban streets to Grandma's. The bay window was empty and dark: Grandma always used to put the same old moulting Christmas tree in the window, festooned with two sets of lights and tie-on chocolates that she called 'fancies'. The ends of the branches were bald from when Alice and Nick were little and had tugged the chocolates off and stripped the soft plastic needles with them. When Mum offered to buy her a new tree Grandma had said, 'It'll see me out,' and Alice had been glad. It wouldn't have been the same with a new leafy tree.

She carried the apple mush round the back and emptied it out near the hedge, where it could rot down in peace and put some goodness back into the soil. At least something would come from it; unlike her relationship with Danny. Nothing was going to come from that. Why couldn't she just have the strength of mind to turn her stupid phone off?

When Alice finally unlocked the back door and stepped into Grandma's silent house, it wasn't possible to keep going. The atmosphere in the house had set; the mingled smells of chip fat and disinfectant and Vick had congealed in the cold, into a medium it was barely possible to push your way through. Alice leant over the sink and forced the window open, then sat at the kitchen table. She stared down at her feet and saw there was a sticky teaspoon lying on the floor. Her Dad hadn't been here once. That was her Mum's complaint: his own parents' house and he hadn't even been once in six months. She remembered coming here when she was little, how the warm air smelt of baking and her Grandma was flicking the cat off the table with a tea towel, while the radio chattered and Grandpa was playing the piano and singing *Old Man River* in the front room and Grandma was rolling her eyes and saying 'You can't hear yourself think!' and Alice was begging 'Can I help you ice the cake? Please? Please?' and Grandma was laughing and lifting her onto the chair for a cuddle.

Hot tears sprang to Alice's eyes. Of course Dad hadn't been here. How could he bear it? Alice glimpsed down a tunnel in her head, herself, twenty-five years on, forcing her way into Mum and Dad's empty house. Facing the mess, having to sort it.

Why would you go there? What could you possibly hope to find?

The lives that had been lived here at Grandma's, they'd had their moments. There were smiles in the photos, music sheets in the piano stool, once-brilliant daubs of hers and Nick's magnetted to the fridge door. There were ingredients for Grandma's fantastic almond cakes in the kitchen cupboards; now stale, sour, grey. Crawling with silverfish. The good things were already gone. Nothing could be saved. Her father must have known this.

She could see that you would be ashamed. But it would be like being ashamed of wetting your pants. Ashamed that you couldn't help it. Ashamed that it had come to this, to old age and dirt; ashamed that you hadn't been here every day, washing things; ashamed that Grandma wouldn't let you buy her anything new; ashamed that she had refused a cleaner and sacked the home help and told the community health nurse to fuck off, and that you had been powerless to stop her, and that everything was broken and dirty; ashamed that nothing you had done had stemmed the rising tide of decay.

Alice imagined seeing her Dad (who was in hospital, who she hadn't even visited yet, for god's sake) and liking and understanding him. Instead of being impatient with the irritating old buffer of her mother's complaints. She blew her nose and gathered herself and went slowly up to the bedroom. The bed looked OK. Not all that old, really – a bit Charles Rennie Mackintosh. Quite designer-y. She dragged the stained mattress to the floor, where it blocked the door and she had to battle on all fours to roll it over onto itself. The sour stench and floppy dead weight of it were almost welcome. All those tiny flakes of sloughed skin; she was practically rolling up her grandparents' bodies. It was the least she could do. She wedged it by the chest of drawers and fetched a knife from the kitchen drawer to unscrew the bed frame. But the screws were stuck fast, the blade broke before a single one had loosened.

The bedhead was weirdly sticky to touch; from medicine, Alice supposed, or from honey and lemon drinks, or breakfasts in bed. Or even, a million years ago, her grandparents' sexual secretions? She tried to unthink the thought. Abandoning her broken knife she searched under the stairs for a toolbox, then went out into the sweet fresh air to the DIY on the corner. There was a product you could use for loosening stuff; Danny had sprayed it on her bike lock when it had jammed. It was true, he used to be kind. When was the last time he was kind? She fought back tears.

The balding man in the DIY refused to understand what she wanted. 'In a can - you spray it on, it loosens things.'

'Lubricant, you mean?'

'Yes, for screws.'

'Lubricant for screws.'

To Alice's humiliation, a spurt of laughter escaped her.

'WD40,' said the man. 'Here. What kind of a screwdriver are you using?'

'A normal one.' How could he know about the knife?

'What you want is one of these. Best screwdriver a girl could have.' He wiggled his toilet-brush eyebrows and handed her a heavy metal-handled tool with a price sticker that said £22.50.

'I – why is it better?'

'Does all the work for you. All you need's apply a little pressure. See?' He demonstrated a little switch in the handle. 'Up for screwing. Down for unscrewing. Turns itself around, see?'

She didn't see but it was pretty obvious she needed the best tool for the job, since the bed probably hadn't been taken to bits for fifty years. And the sooner she got out of this lecher's shop the better. She crossed her fingers and gave him her visa card.

Having duly sprayed all the screws she tried to use the screwdriver. But when she leant on it, as Mr Lech had demonstrated, the handle twizzled round uselessly while the head remained motionless. The only way to make it work was to put the little switch in the central position, which turned it into an ordinary screwdriver. But it was big and clumsy to hold and all her force could not budge a single screw.

Alice fell back against the folded mattress. Something, one single thing, surely, had to go right this weekend. Dispassionately she wondered what it would be. She pressed her Christmas angel badge and watched it flashing for a while. Such daylight as there was had almost drained from the sky and she got up and switched on the lights. She was starving. What were the options? Mum would be going straight from the library to hospital because Alice had the car. Who could she ask to help her? There was no one. Head wanted the trailer back tomorrow. If she hadn't had to deal with his wretched apples she'd have finished hours ago. To have done all this and still no bed – it was beyond enduring.

In a rage she snatched up the screwdriver and attacked the screws again – heaving, twisting – and was at last rewarded by an infinitesimal give, then movement. Slowly, grudgingly, the screws at the top end began to yield. She loosened them all then moved on to the foot. The problem would come in removing them; the whole frame would collapse, probably onto her. It was already listing drunkenly to one side. Her phone went and she crawled to her bag to get it. Not Danny. Of course not: wrong ring tone. Mum, from the bus, wanting to know if she could pick her up from the hospital at eight-thirty. 'Probably Mum, but I'm just in the middle of this. I'll text you, OK?' Her mother wondered plaintively what they could eat. 'Apple sauce,' she said meanly and hung up. Danny would be cooking his disgusting onion-and-baked-bean omelette, which he made whenever she asked him to cook so she wouldn't ask him again. She thought bitterly of the delicious things she'd cooked for him from her Jamie Oliver book. He said they'd got boring. It was him that was boring. Not her. *Him.* She had a brainwave. The frame could be balanced on kitchen chairs, one each side. The seats were too high but when she laid them on their backs it was just possible to slide them under so the frame rested on their legs. She fetched a cup to put the screws in.

Piece by piece she carried the frame downstairs. The bed-head was unwieldy; it caught a couple of the pictures above the stairs as she tried to angle it round the top banister. Tough. Nobody would miss them. The glass crunched into the carpet as she trudged up and down the stairs. At last all the pieces of the bed were in the hall. She emptied the screws into the glove compartment and began loading the bed into the trailer. Header. Footer. Side frame. Side frame. Top frame. Bottom frame. Slats. The wood was dense and heavy, probably some precious, endangered-species, non-renewable hardwood.

She slumped into the driver's seat, trembling with hunger and fatigue. As she pulled away from the kerb she heard the wood slither and rattle into position. She should have brought something to pad it where it leant against the sides of the trailer. Well there was plenty of cloth in Grandma's house – old sheets, towels? No. She couldn't bear to stop. It would be alright. She was driving so slowly and carefully that it would hardly shift at all, there probably wouldn't be a scratch on it. She made herself keep her eyes on the speedometer – don't go above twenty.

Then her phone started up. *Danny Boy.* He had selected the ringtone for her. Well, tough. It was too late. She didn't want to speak to him. She glanced at the speedometer, twenty mph. She didn't allow her eyes even a flicker towards the phone. She looked straight back to the road. There was an angel.

An angel. Life size. White in her headlights. She hit the brake.

A lot of things happened at once, and it was only possible to itemise them afterwards. The angel stretched out her white wings as if she would fly. Alice's seat belt ripped into her neck and shoulder like a bear-claw, while the car tried to pitch her through the windscreen then jerked madly backwards. There was a long noise, shockingly loud, of crashing and splintering. A man running to the flight-poised angel. Then pounding silence, expanding like a mushroom cloud in her head.

The man's face loomed at Alice's window. The silence popped. 'Are you alright? Please, let me.' He opened the door. 'Can you get out? You – you stopped – like that!'

Alice fumbled at her seat belt and slithered out of the car. She saw that the trailer was on its side in the road and that pieces of bed were scattered everywhere.

'Here,' said the man. 'You've had a shock. Come and sit down.' He led her into a lit doorway and spoke a different language to some other people who went outside and began to move the trailer. He sat her and the angel on a sofa and went into the kitchen to make a cup of tea.

Alice could see now that it was a child, not an angel. She had on a white dress, intricately embroidered at neck and hem. Her brown face was solemn and her black eyes examined Alice minutely. She looked about four years old. After a moment she slid off the sofa and picked up a bowl of sweets from the table. She carried it carefully to Alice, and offered it to her. Alice took a gold-wrapped toffee.

The man came back with two mugs of tea. 'I'm so sorry. It's her birthday. She was dancing when her cousins left, I forgot to lock the door.'

The little girl stretched out her arms again as if she would do a twirl, then noticed Alice watching her and concentrated very hard on choosing a sweet from the bowl.

'Her mother,' the man said quietly, 'she runs out looking for her mother.'

'Her mother?'

He brushed his hand across his eyes. 'She's not here.' Alice saw him gather himself into politeness. 'I am so sorry. I'll pay for your trailer, your firewood. I don't know how to thank you. You saved her life.'

The man's face was beautiful. The child's face was beautiful.

'It wasn't firewood. It was a bed.'

'Ah. I will pay for a new bed. Of course.'

The child, whom she had thought was an angel, was alive and gravely unpeeling a mini-mars bar. Slowly, with the tinny taste of the tea, feeling began to creep back into Alice's numbed body and soul. She had not killed the child. She had saved the child. The beautiful man was smiling at her.

The feeling creeping through her was happiness.

'That bed was a lost cause,' she said. 'I'm glad your little girl is safe.'

Conspiracy

Eleanor Knight

'Sorry. Could you close the window?'

Why I apologised I do not know. My bare legs were splayed in the stirrups and I awaited stitches. The baby screamed and slithered in the arms of someone who was trying to weigh it.

Ten yards away in the car-park (we were on the ground floor) a man stood, looking in, a cigarette between his lips.

'Feeling a bit chilly are we?' asked the midwife, a blow-in from Tyrone. 'That's quite normal.'

'Bit of fresh air never goes amiss,' said Miss Cunningham from below. Beside her on the trolley lay the episiotomy scissors.

'Over in a jiffy,' she grinned.

'It's just that there's a man out there,' I said '– and he can see everything.'

The man had let his cigarette fall to the ground and was rolling it beneath his foot. I waved. He waved back.

'Open or closed?' asked the midwife, Kelly, her hand on the swing frame.

'Closed', said Miss Cunningham through clenched teeth. I imagine she was threading the needle. 'Mum knows best.'

'Oh but it's Ron!' said Kelly, hesitating.

'Ron from the morgue?' The consultant's voice was slightly muffled.

'No, no. Not any more. No, Ron's in orthopaedics now...'

'Then what's he doing over here? Orthopaedics is in the Millennium Wing.'

At the words Millennium Wing, both women rolled their eyes.

'Take some nice deep breaths with the gas and air now,' said Miss Cunningham, and then 'Swab, Kelly.'

Kelly twizzled away from the window with the gaiety of a cheerleader. She didn't shut it.

'Poor Ron...'

'All the Irish women I ever meet are midwives or journalists,' I said, happily.

A fortnight later, having finally got out of my dressing gown (the baby suffered from colic and I from debilitatingly morbid thoughts concerning it, teenagers, and the urban slag-heap of builders' rubble at the end of the street) I walked out to the supermarket, taking the baby in the sling. I wasn't, you understand, ready to put him in a trolley seat and parade him down the aisles where he would be fingered by the toffee-probing digits of old ladies, or encounter toddlers who hit him in the face with Tellytubbies they had sucked.

I filled the trolley with good things: exotic fruits, salads rich and green as the Kulu valley, pillows of warm white bread. I also bought biscuits I thought my mother would like, salmon fillet and some sanitary pads, the kind that can be stitched into a thick, winter quilt as the nights draw in.

Reaching the check-out, I pulled my recycled carrier bags from the trolley and put them on the conveyor belt. There was Ron.

'Hello!' he said. 'You've got that all sewn up!'

I glanced at his badge – 'Hello I'm Ron'.

'I beg your pardon?'

'All sewn up. Your bags. All taken care of. Sorry. You don't sew up a bag, do you? Better to say you've got it all in the bag.'

'But you haven't scanned the items and placed them in the bagging area yet,' I said, a little impatiently. I was on maternity leave from my job as editor of an in-house supermarket training magazine.

'Right. Then I'll count how many bags you use as we go along and award you your points at the end accordingly.'

'Interesting,' I said, 'Nobody ever says accordingly in that sentence.'

'It's a new suggestion from our training magazine.

They're really livening it up these days.'

'I see,' I said.

When he got to the sanitary towels he held them aloft, nodding to the woman behind me in the queue who was waiting with four bottles of champagne and a tub of low fat margarine. She looked at her watch.

'Ever so brave you know,' said Ron. 'Tough as anything. Grew up on a farm.'

The woman smiled, as indulgently as her proposed haste would allow.

'How did you know that?' I asked.

'It comes up on your loyalty card. Look.' He swivelled the little screen around on its plastic neck. I read aloud, 'Jane Fairbrother. Date of birth 19th October 1978. Tonsillectomy 1983. Form prize for French 1985, favourite dish rice pudding, favourite game cat's cradle... '

He scrolled down the screen where listed were my first three sexual partners and a letter I'd sent to my MP when I was eleven.

'I'd forgotten all about cat's cradle,' I said.

My mother came for tea. She wrapped the baby in a shawl she'd knitted, worried he was too hot and unwrapped him again. She did this five times by my reckoning, although she could have fitted another one in while I was in the lavatory.

'Just like your father!' she said. This was hard to deny as apart from the glasses they were identical.

She was gathering her things to go when the doorbell rang.

'I'll get it!' she sang, waddling down the narrow corridor of our maisonette with her coat half-on.

'Have you considered the promises of Jesus?' I recognised the voice immediately. Ron's.

'Not now, thank you,' said my mother. 'My daughter became agnostic at university, although she doesn't care to discuss it with me. I'm C of E.'

'How's she coping?' asked Ron, in a whisper that got a small avalanche underway in the Cairngorms.

'As well as can be expected, dear. You never know where you are with the first one, and neither do they. Hopeless!

Still,' she said stepping redoubtably out onto the path, 'they say the first twenty years are the worst. Goodbye Jane, darling! See you next Thursday.'

I am thirty, still an only child, and we had just arranged to meet on Wednesday.

At my six week check I sat in the GP's waiting room reading a magazine about the elastic return to form of the celebrity midriff. I looked for a whole minute at Catherine Zeta Jones before and after and realised that although her waist seemed actually to have shrunk since the birth of her son, it was only because her breasts had swollen to nearly twice their original size. Look on my works ye mighty and despair, I thought, as a trickle of foremilk pooled in my bra.

Ron came over.

'Hullo.' His side-burns were dark and greasy, a coach driver from a pit town, though he lacked the sardonic charm.

'These'll come in handy,' he said, reaching into his dufflebag and pulling out a box of breastpads.

'We swore by nipple shields,' said a man from behind the *Economist*. 'Plastic. Cracked nipples are a nightmare.' He winced and shook his head, sorrowfully.

'Never mind, love,' said an elderly chap in a north eastern dialect I will not presume to imitate, 'You only have to keep it up for six months these days. Look on the bright side,' is what I think he was saying, 'I bet you've an appetite on you like a horse.'

This has always puzzled me, the confusion between 'eats like a horse' and 'I could eat a horse.' My father-in-law eats like a horse, but only inasmuch as he eats practically nothing but muesli.

'Jane Fairbrother?' The GP appeared amongst us, a young Asian woman, Dr Amit, who had shrunk still further since last time I saw her, possibly as a result of a punitive dietary regime she would hesitate to recommend to her patients. 'This way please.'

'And you feel quite well in yourself?' Dr Amit asked as she tidied away her instruments. 'Everything back to normal? Bowels? Waterworks? That reminds me, did you bring a sample?'

I took it from my bag as she slid open a hatch in the wall. Ron's head appeared in the aperture and his hand shot through to receive the warm phial before they were both lost from view and the hatch was sealed.

I stared at the wall.

'Everything alright?'

'Ron,' I said.

Dr Amit rapped on the hatch and there he was again.

'Patient wants a word,' she said, in a voice that intimated 'Watch it Ron, a few days in the lab do not constitute substantive medical training.'

'No... ' I said, 'I didn't want to talk to him, I just wanted... ' She closed the hatch with a smile of satisfaction.

'I wanted to ask you,' I faltered, 'I knew it would be him. I knew it would be Ron.'

'Of course it's Ron. He's pathology.'

'He was in the waiting room when I arrived.'

She fixed her smile like a lemon meringue pie.

'He was in the supermarket... He came to my home.'

'Oh no, Ron doesn't do doorstep. That's the area team. They have a van.'

'He was in the car park at the beginning.'

'Not Ron, they don't let him drive.'

A tear dropped from my cheek onto the baby's head. Dr Amit swivelled her chair towards her screen.

'OK.' She tapped the keyboard. 'Iron tablets. Are you taking them? Ah... no.' She ran the cursor down the screen. 'Keith Beveridge, Lavender Gardens SW11, advised you on the 73 bus that iron tablets cause constipation and as a result you stopped taking them. Correct?'

'Well, yes... I... '

'Did you not wonder why he was on the 73 if he lives in Battersea?'

'I had no idea.'

'Of course not.' Lemon meringue. 'It also says here that Jim Plooges advised you to buy an expensive liquid supplement from the health food shop.'

'Jim Plooges?'

'I know. It's French, originally. His mother's Scottish,

hence Jim.' She leaned towards me with a clean tissue, my tears flowed freely now and I took it gratefully. 'Oh Jane,' she said, 'It's what we're here for. The NHS.'

She watched me with her palms on her knees, an attitude that has been found to appear unthreatening to all sectors of the community. A suicide bomber might be advised to sit like this before pressing the button.

'Are you having morbid thoughts?'

'What, now? Can you tell?' I shuffled in my chair, blew my nose and did my best to wipe my face, putting myself in order for fear that Ron should appear again at any moment and offer his sympathies.

'People offer advice all the time. Men...' I tried to explain.

'Well,' said Dr Amit, simply, 'It should come as no surprise to you that other people have some experience of it all,' she glanced at her screen, scrolling away, 'even if you... oh dear..' There it was: the D for biology A level. She passed another tissue. 'Look. It's quite normal you know, for feelings of – we won't call it paranoia, yet – of anxiety, disquiet. After childbirth.'

I sniffed, nodding.

'Some people find joining a club can help, a hobby. Do you know, it's funny but there's a study that found depression less likely to occur in those who regularly practise a religion.'

'Have you been talking to my mother?'

'No, no.' She laughed, making a nylon noise by rubbing her skirt over her tights. 'It's in the *Lancet*.' She passed me her copy.

'A pointed surgical knife with two sharp edges,' I said, weakly, as the baby's fist patted steadily at my cardigan in a tiny but persistent appeal.

I stood up to go.

'Perhaps we should just touch on contraception... ?' said Dr Amit.

'It's too late,' I said, 'I have a baby.'

Over the months that followed I saw Ron on several occasions, the most notable being the last. I was at the wedding reception of an old school friend when Ron appeared in a white tuxedo with a large tray of canapés on his shoulder.

'Thank you, Ron,' I said, taking a snippet of toast with parma ham (the baby was with my mother). Ron bowed politely but was nudged by a bridesmaid making an emotional exit, and the canapés fell, inevitably, ham-side down.

I turned quickly away from the scene, Ron on all fours, apologising, scraping up the debris at the feet of a Queen's Guardsman and trying – and I really believe I saw him do this – to arrange what he had salvaged attractively on the platter, before realising that the speed of removal was paramount. I drank a glass of champagne and danced a quickstep with the bride's father, a navy man, retired.

'What have you been getting up to lately?' he asked, in genuine ignorance. The news of my firstborn delighted him just as much as would one of his own and I was invited to 'bring the whole family down' next time I was in Sussex, or wherever it was he lived.

I never returned to my job on the magazine. I worked freelance until I gave birth to twin girls, highly competitive red-heads with a shared passion for rock-climbing.

As I said, I didn't see Ron again, neither did I ever find out why he was taken off the morgue.

Café Bohemia

Alison MacLeod

Do any of the following apply to you? (Answer yes or no.)

The owner of the small café shrugs, as if to say if you don't like it, you know where the door is. I stare at the green form she has pulled from the napkin dispenser. I wasn't expecting a visa waiver.

The form is rectangular and about seven inches long. It has boxes that require ticks. Each box looks like a small trap-door. But the woman who wears a badge that reads 'Zlata' is shaking her index finger. It appears too delicate, too elegant, for the rest of her. 'Forget box! Answer!' She heaves up the sloping mass of her breasts and adjusts her hair-net. She smells of patchouli oil. It seems unlikely that she is English. I am not certain that she is a she.

How can I explain about words, answers and me? If I am lucky, they obey as they exit my mouth. If I'm not, they are like dogs that have been let off the lead.

'A cup of tea, please.' I haul up my jeans and try to steady my voice. I have not used it yet today, and am conscious it sounds like a rusting pulley struggling to raise the empty bucket of me.

My cheeks are waxy white from the rain blowing off the seafront. Outside, there's a gale-force wind that could strip the skin from a small animal. The café windows shudder. Zlata stares. She knows why I've come. She passes me the form, a pen and the back of a paper menu. 'Words! No strangers here.'

'It's a café,' I try.

But she will have seen me outside, staring at the Room-For-Rent sign in the window.

Let me be clear. Café Bohemia is not only without pretension, it is without hope. It is without coffee, croissants, biscotti, sticky buns, chocolate sprinkles, frothy milk, newspapers or stir-sticks. It is without charm, tablecloths, carnations in small vases, candles in Chianti bottles, literary types or franchise dreams. There is tea. There are five bare tables and a yellowing linoleum floor. The walls are marked by continents of damp. A dried and twisted Palm-Sunday frond is taped to the wall above the door, next to a clock whose hands are stuck at eight minutes past twelve. A framed magazine picture of a field of Sussex poppies dips on the far wall, but the glass is gone and the splashes of red have been bleached by the glaring years. The three large windows offer a view of St. James's Street you'd turn away from if you could – a view of fogged-up buses, sodden shopping bags, and cyclists who strain uphill against the elements.

I try to smile, imitating the ease of a regular. 'Milk, two sugars, please.' I need a haircut. Rain still trickles down my neck. My clothes were wet even before the rain, wet when I pulled them from the dryer at the launderette. I ran out of change. I have hardly slept since I closed the door on my mother's house and stumbled down the steps.

Outside, two couples run headlong past the café's windows, cowering beneath a single oversized umbrella. I long to be one of them, my arm clutching the waist of a loved one – or, failing that, to be stepping in front of ten tons of bus, all longing flattened.

Zlata's mouth puckers with impatience. My eyes spasm slightly in their sockets. I nod at last to the sign in the window. The empty bucket of me sways on the line. 'I wanted to ask…' In my mind's eye, I can still see the scrawled words that seduced me on my way uphill. The felt-tip letters were smeared by condensation, but the words were legible enough: ROOMS FOR RENT.

At one of the tables, a man with a withered leg and a boarded-up window of a face looks my way. He is already writing. Will he take the last room? I can't risk it.

I glance at the piece of paper Zlata has pushed across the counter-top. 'Welcome to the United States. I-94W Nonimmigrant Visa Waiver/Arrival Departure Record.'

I have no immediate desire to enter the United States. I am in Brighton, England, a popular seaside resort – the haunt of clandestine lovers, sentimental criminals, thrill-seekers and failed artists. But I want the room. I need the room. I take a seat at a table. My rival hauls his leg close. Zlata brings me stewed tea in a chunky white mug. She stares pointedly at the dirt beneath my nails. Not dirt, I want to say. Ash. Or, strictly speaking, not ash. Cremains.

A. Do you have a communicable disease; physical or mental disorder, or are you a drug user or addict?

When I was twelve, my kite landed in the canopy of the elm outside the family semi. 'Eliot! Eliot!' called my mother. 'Not so high!' She was on her knees, a slave always to herbaceous borders and garden beds.

I had my hand on the tail of my kite when the world rushed up, I sailed down and my head hit the pavement next to the rubbish bins.

We learned that day that eye-hand coordination is not my strong suit. Although my special needs report assures me I am a medium-to-high-functioning autistic, those heights, regrettably do not extend to tree canopies.

The kite came down by itself.

I am not simple. Far from it. I was classified as 'articulate' in the transferable-skills test, which, like Form I-94W, favoured boxes of the trap-door variety. In fact, it is my belief that the early blow to my head left me with a skewed but heightened ability, not only to retain words of all kinds, but to feel them – written words particularly. Sometimes, I cannot un-feel the words for days.

Take the news story on the weekend. I managed to read it as I often do, over an anonymous shoulder, without buying the paper, in Tesco Express.

It reported an explosion – *my eardrums, my eyes – birds shriek into flight* – in Iraq. Thirty were killed. Firemen – *flaming men* – rushed to the scene but ran out of petrol as they crossed the city. Each man is paid only £15 per month but they often have to club together to buy the petrol so they can go where they are needed. Sometimes, there is not enough water for the hoses – *I wank but I cannot come.* They arrived to bodies only –

95

dead weights, souls shuttered. One of the crew struggled – *the ground slippery with blood* – out of the rubble bearing the final victim, but the body was not all there so the man returned, under the threat of gas leaks and collapsing concrete – *radiance streaming through the dust* – to find the missing leg and hand – *hold me.*

I do not take offence when people murmur that, like the exploded man, I am not all there. They have a point. In spite of my ability to write in complete sentences, in life, I am distracted. I panic when I approach escalators I cannot remember to wear a belt. I find ordinary speech with others a terrible dance. Apparently, I do not read the signs of human emotion and social intercourse very well. (It follows that intercourse of all kinds is infrequent.) Perhaps that is why I prefer to work with those who also are not all there. The dead do not murmur.

I have learned it is inappropriate to remark – at bus-stops, in the queue at Tesco's, around the community bonfire for the homeless – that organs and soft tissues vapourise at 760 to 1,150 degrees Fahrenheit.

My job is to empty the cooling tray. It is careful work. The cooling tray contains the remnants, remnants that are not the ashes but the bone fragments of limbs that once danced, ran, had intercourse and flew kites. I empty the tray into the cremulator, or the electric cremated remains processor. Hit the switch and the cremulator pulverises, like any good kitchen Braun. I tip the contents of the cremulator into a heavy-duty ziplock bag. I weigh it. If the job has been well executed at each stage, I will finish with approximately three percent of that body's original mass. Or to talk shop, the cremains.

At the crematorium, we are mindful of labels and procedures. It is a limited system I manage well. I am good on systems. However, what the crematorium manager, Ray, will not explain to the loved ones is that you can never get all of one body out of the furnace's chamber before the next body is entered.

In our final incarnation, we are each bigger – or more – than ourselves. We are a smattering of others – us plus some – and perhaps we all need that: to be more than merely all there.

Mother bought the scarf from the *Past Times* catalogue. 1930s 'Art Nouveau' style, she said. We stared as she pulled it from its cardboard envelope. She pulled and pulled. It was very long. When she wrapped it around her neck, I told her she looked like a lady in a country garden.

I never knew she knew how to tie a reliable knot.

The police were shuffling from foot to foot in our front room when I arrived home. I don't know how they got in. They let me look. They told me they were not allowed to touch. Someone else was on his way; he was allowed to touch. I thought of the last time I had touched my mother. I'd lifted her hair free where it was trapped by the scarf.

She chose the garage so I wouldn't be left with the image as I made my breakfast or hoovered her room.

But I see her still, suspended like a question mark in mid-air.

A woman of sixty-two. People think you make it to a certain age and the decent thing is to avoid unpleasantness. But I believe she'd had her fill of pleasantness: of flowers, tidy borders and the monthly support group for parents of middle-aged children like me - Tea, biscuits and 'tards.

I could not stay. I ran down the steps with only loose change in my pockets.

An anagram of 'room for rent' is 'frret no moor'.

I require only a hotplate, a wash-basin and a lock on my door.

I am used to communal facilities.

I use a good nail-brush daily.

B. Have you ever been arrested or convicted for an offense or a crime involving moral turpitude; or are you seeking to engage in criminal or immoral activities?

It is true that I masturbate frequently.

It is also true that I sometimes pocket the gleanings I sieve from the cooling tray. The gleanings are the melted lumps of metal left behind by gold teeth, fillings, jewellery that's been missed, coins on eyes, casket hinges, belt buckles, underwire support bras, metal plates and hip replacements. On its way to the furnace, the coffin passes through a magnetic field but it's far from foolproof, and even if it bleeps, who will pull a gold tooth from a dead man?

Simpler to wait it out.

There's a law against selling on the precious metal found in the cooling tray but the thing I like about Ray is that he turns a blind eye, as if to say finders, keepers.

Zlata, you have the look of a woman whose teeth know the softness of precious metal from scrap. My deposit for the room is rolling in my pockets.

Frret no moor.

That was the revelation on my uphill journey. Revelation, dizzying and pure.

But I have reason to fret. To fret moor. I am concerned the authorities will take exception to these words, which I have now committed to paper. They will have their instructions and this confession. They will have my retina-scans and my fingerprints on the tea mug. They will have their dogs who will smell the stink of immorality in my coat pockets.

Look. The man who was also writing is gone. Vanished. I didn't hear him go, and him with a dead leg.

That is the thing, I suppose. You never hear anyone go.

C. Have you ever been or are you now involved in espionage or sabotage; or in terrorist activities; or genocide; or between 1933 and 1945 were you involved, in any way, in persecutions associated with Nazi Germany or its allies?

It happens, literally, in the blinking of an eye. The blindfold grips me. The pen falls from my hand.

'Zlata?' I whisper.

The knot is tight at the back of my head. I don't understand. I hear the sounds of feet – 'Who's there?' – and am led across the floor, through a door and up the stairs. The scent of patchouli oil is strong. My bowels loosen. In my mind's eye, I see myself left crouching, cold and alone, in the darkness; I gag on a jetstream of water; my fingernails are pulled from the nailbeds.

Have I incriminated myself? The words repeat on me. Do any of the following diseases – pox, genital warts, sleeping sickness – apply to you or to any of your allies? (Answer yes or no.) Between 1933 and 1945 – *There'll be blue birds over* – were you in mental disarray or in Nazi Germany? (At the crematorium, we are mindful of labels and procedures.) Have you ever been arrested or convicted for an offense or an addiction relating to kites or flying high? Have you ever been or are you now involved in espionage at newspaper kiosks? In genocide? (I use a good nailbrush. In my line of work, it's important.) Or in terrorist activities? Welcome to the United—

I am spun around. My lungs are like dying balloons. A baton of some sort is placed into my hand and I hear merry applause. 'Hit!' shouts Zlata. 'Hit high!'

Is my opponent very tall? The fight-or-flight instinct surges belatedly within me. I strike out. I beat the air and lose my balance, tumbling into a stranger's body. Laughter breaks around me, the laughter of many, a crowd. I have heard of these games. Soon I will be stripped naked. My opponent bides his time as I bash the darkness. From somewhere, I hear the unscrewing of bottle tops, the popping of a cork. Drinks are poured as I reel. When my baton strikes something overhead, 'Encore!' cry the onlookers.

I take aim and strike again.

Shrapnel rains down from above. I cover my head with my arms and cower.

The blindfold is torn from my head. 'Surprise!' shouts Zlata. I blink upwards. A smiling, broken piñata dangles, gutted. Green confetti and brightly wrapped sweets lay scattered on the floor at my feet.

'Many are the broken here,' intones Zlata.

I try to breathe. 'Does that mean you still have a room for rent?'

Behind me, the boarded up man with the dead leg lounges on the sofa with a woman in a blue sequinned dress. She'd look like a film star if it weren't for the rash of needle marks on her forearms. In the corner, a louring artist, wearing only his underwear, contemplates a canvas that leans up against a window. A shabby man with an aristocratic voice tries to woo Zlata with sweets he has scooped from the floor. A woman tunes a ukulele while debating the price of sea bass with a man in Coke-bottle specs. There are others – too many for the communal sitting room. How is it possible that we – this great, motley crowd – are here, just one storey up from the hopeless, one-room café?

On the wall I notice a duplicate of the picture downstairs: the Sussex fields, the poppies blowing. Only here, the poppies glow a rich red. The palm-Sunday frond above the door is fresh and green. I see that Zlata's guests use Form I-94W as paper napkins for their salted peanuts and pretzels. A few smoke it in roll-up fashion. When I examine the green confetti on the floor, I realise that it too was once Form I-94W.

'This way,' Zlata commands. 'I will show you your room.'

I have been granted asylum.

The same Sunday-supplement poppies hang on my wall. I test the single bed, too short for my feet but reassuringly firm. There is a wash basin and a tooth mug, though my teeth are all my own, and there is a wardrobe without a door. There is also, to my relief, a nail brush. Death will not cling to me here.

Zlata and I both go quiet. In the sitting room, someone is reciting W.H. Someone's poem 'Lullaby'.

Yes, I could sleep. I could lie down now and sleep like a child in a truckle-bed.

I spot a door behind the wardrobe. 'Why not?' says Zlata, nodding like a sibyl. 'Yes! Go! See.'

I push the wardrobe out of my way. The door is a poor, sticky fit but it gives way under my weight. I find myself in a room identical to my own, right down to the picture, the tooth mug, the nail brush – and the ill-fitting door at the back. It leads to another. And it, to another.

I gather speed. I race past a man asleep in his bed; for a moment, he appears pregnant, the mound of his belly steep beneath the sheet. In the next room, I excuse myself to a pretty girl who is conjugating verbs by the window. Then I discover an elderly man on his knees on a prayer mat, and next door to him, a boy who is scribbling equations on the wall with a stubby pencil. If I am strange, I am not, it would seem, a stranger.

Each room gives way impossibly to the next and that room, to another. Occasionally, I arrive at a loo – 'I beg your pardon!' – but Zlata's accommodation is seemingly without end. Believe me. Hours have passed, and I am not yet at the edges of the territory that is Café Bohemia.

I have met no border guards, reaction teams or sniffer dogs.

Distantly, I hear the music of those words still… *Eye and knocking heart may bless…* Dum dum dum dum dum. Dum dum dum dum dum dum. *Nights of insult let you pass.* Dum dum dum-dum-dum dum-dum dum. The poem is everywhere.

Cuckoo

Nicholas Royle

Swift stepped down from the train in the dark suit that his ex-wife, Maggie, had often joked was his writer's outfit, but really, what else could he wear? He waited on the platform for a moment while the other travellers headed towards the exit. The train departed and was soon no more than a dot in the distance. Swift took off his glasses and cleaned them using the duster he kept neatly folded in his notebook. Once he felt the stillness of the empty platform settling around him, he lifted his bag on to his shoulder.

On his way out of the station, he stopped by a piece of public art: a poem printed on a board fixed to the wall. It was a poem about the large station clock that was suspended above the platform. Swift had always maintained that as a novelist he was unqualified to judge poetry, but he silently congratulated the poet for her description of the clock's 'poker face and sorrowful hands'. In 1978, he read, the great clock's mechanical workings had been replaced by an electrical mechanism, which had evidently been a poor and inadequate substitute.

> *They say it was the water getting in*
> *That stopped it dead at half past three*
> *But I say it had had enough*
> *Of that cuckoo nesting deep within*[1]

He walked on, allowing himself no more than a glance at the tearooms where a celebrated film had once been shot.

---

[1] Extract from 'Stations of the Clock' by Lynne Alexander.

Leaving the station, he looked at his watch. There was time before the reading, not only to visit the bookshop, but to walk around the town. He had deliberately caught an early train. As he crossed the small car park, a woman passed him from left to right. He did a double take. The chestnut bob, the pale skin at the back of the neck. The way she held her head slightly downturned, even the hurried walk, leaning forward. The woman got into a car, started its engine and drove directly out of the car park.

It wasn't her, but it looked like her.

It couldn't have been her.

He, too, left the car park and looked both ways. He could walk left over the railway bridge and out into open countryside, or right, up the slight incline towards the crossroads at the centre of the town. That way lay the venue for the reading, but there was plenty of time.

Faint screams reached his ears, prompting him to raise his pointed chin. Sickle-shaped birds scratched at the forget-me-not sky. Swifts, *apus apus*, harbingers of summer. (They were early this year, as they had been the year before and the year before that.) Even when associated with summer, 'harbinger' carried a brooding undertone. Had he ever used the word, Swift wondered? He had read recently that the swift population was declining because of a shortage of nesting sites. Almost invariably they nested in old buildings, in the eaves or in holes in the brickwork, and as more and more of these were fixed up or barred with pigeon netting, so the swift was rendered homeless.

Not that they spent that much time in their nests. The swift lived more of its life on the wing than any other bird – feeding, drinking, mating, even sleeping during flight. But with no nesting sites there would be no young and with no young eventually there would be no birds at all.

Swift had made it his business to find out about the swift.

The legs of the swift were very short, little used, almost vestigial. A grounded bird would often find itself marooned and never fly again.

Their piercing cries were supposed to symbolise the screaming of lost souls.

He walked up the hill, where a toy shop caught his eye. Among the brightly coloured boxes of board games and packs of cards was a display of model animals that made his breath catch in his throat. These were not the cheaply made, roughly moulded plastic models he had got used to seeing over the years whenever he had looked in a toyshop window or taken a shortcut across the toy floor of a department store – made in the Far East, with more of an eye to profit than for detail. These, instead, were the models he had played with as a boy. The same make. He recognised the tiny painted hooves of the farmyard goat, the resplendent mane of the roaring lion, the erect gorilla with its fists in the air.

Swift had always liked small towns. He had always thought the phrase 'small-town mentality' unfair to them with their family-run shops and their pavements and squares that were gathering places for friends and neighbours. He lived in the city, where rest was impossible. There was always a deadline to meet, a reading to get to, a book to finish, the next one to start.

Swift's feet never touched the ground.

Next door to the toyshop, a window filled with computers and printers and modems and scanners, and at the heart of this display of the very latest hardware a big beautiful old typewriter. Swift wondered if the tug of familiarity was just a tiny bit specific. The machine reminded him of the one on which he had composed his first novel, the one in which he had written about Agnes.

He remembered the woman in the car park, the vulnerability of the back of her neck. Just like Agnes, whom he had known before Maggie.

There was still time, but he had to make sure he didn't miss the bookshop. His research had told him there was a second-hand bookshop with a decent stock and a good reputation. Swift loved books. He loved reading them, he loved collecting them, he loved sitting on the floor late at night taking them from his shelves at random to gaze at the cover and run his fingers over the title page. Towards the end of his marriage, he had had to start sneaking books into the house.

You'll never read all of these, she'd said.

That wasn't the point, he'd replied.

Swift wondered if Terence loved books – Terence, who had cuckolded Swift – if he read books, if he sat on the floor late at night surrounded by uniform editions of an author's works while the clocks ticked and Maggie breathed slowly in her sleep.

The bookshop was located by the crossroads, which he could now see up ahead where the traffic lights were on red. The bookshop was soon revealed on the other side of the road. The door closed behind him with the tinkle of a bell. Around him were racks of cards and gift books. A sign pointed upstairs. Swift was glad of the handrail as he climbed.

He went where he always went, to paperback fiction. Swift wasn't a serious collector; he collected for pleasure. His eyes grazed the spines, slowing down as he experienced joyous moments of recognition. There was a book he owned. There was another. And another and another and another. This was not unusual; Swift owned a great many books. But perhaps it was unusual that in this grazing he had yet to spot a title that was *not* among his collection. He slowed down and read spine after spine, trailing his finger to aid concentration. He read spine after spine after spine. On this shelf, on this wall, he had them all. He moved to the next wall, authors from H to M. At eye-level were the Ks. Kavan, Kenworthy, Kilworth, Knowles, Kureishi. He had them all. It wasn't just that he owned books by all these authors; he owned these very titles. He started to look for books he didn't have. He searched among Kavan's titles for *The Parson*. They didn't have it. Neither did he.

It was coincidence. He moved across to the shelves on the facing wall. Towards the end of the alphabet. Here too there was nothing he didn't already have. He darted around, dipping in and out of letters, looking for specific authors, for particular types of novel. The Angry Young Men: he had them all, all the ones they had. Experimental novelists: the same ones were here as were on his own shelves at home. He began looking for books from obscure presses, American publishers. Elastic Press, Chronicle Books, Prime Books, Red Hen Press. All present, but only the ones he owned. He looked for rare books. He looked for a book he had once owned and let go and then spent twenty-five years searching for so that he could read it again. He had found it. It, too, was here.

Swift backed out of the room, as if afraid its contents might follow him out, and the handrail took his weight as he descended the staircase. The bell tinkled as he opened the door, but it was a hollow tinkle. He stepped outside. The air was comfortably warm. The distant screams of swifts could still be heard and against them, coming from somewhere beyond the railway station, the unmistakeable spring-time call of the male cuckoo, *cuculus canorus*.

Three uniformed policemen passed by on the opposite side of the road, one of them controlling a black-and-white spaniel by means of a lead and harness with fluorescent trim.

Swift leaned back against the brick wall of the bookshop and took a handkerchief from his pocket with which he wiped his eyes. Then he blew his nose, with a trumpeting flourish. He didn't know if he had ever forgiven Maggie, because she had never asked for his forgiveness. He had always felt slightly lost, since she had left. Like a lost soul, restless.

He started walking back towards the railway station. He had come to regard it, rather than the crossroads, as the centre point, or pivot, of the town, despite the fact it clearly occupied – or possibly created – a marginal, liminal sector in which it, a taxi firm, a pub and a fast-food outlet were the only signs of human activity.

As Swift walked down the incline, he heard loud music approaching at speed. He turned around, frowning at a trapped nerve in his back, to see a souped-up red saloon car decelerating fast as it came level with the bookshop. The driver turned down the volume on his sound system almost to zero as he passed Swift, who was surprised to see him doff his white baseball cap while rolling the car slowly down the hill.

The car had disappeared by the time Swift realised the driver's face had been familiar, but, like a face seen in a dream, it was then impossible to place.

He walked past the car park and started to climb the low bridge over the railway. At the top he stopped and rested his arms on the parapet, from where he could enjoy a view of the station. The policemen who had passed him earlier seemed to be performing a security check of the platforms and railway buildings. The spaniel was still on its lead and was being encouraged to sniff at drains, manhole covers and those little trapdoors that conceal the interior workings of lampposts. Swift wondered what might be going on. There was a gathering of important political leaders taking place in the capital, but that was more than 200 miles away. Could one of them be coming up here at the conclusion of the conference? It seemed unlikely.

Cuck-oo, cuck-oo, cuck-oo.

Swift looked to the west. There was a stand of trees a quarter of a mile away. Then more open land and a wood beyond. Everyone has heard a cuckoo – and its parasitic behaviour is general knowledge – yet relatively few have ever seen one.

Turning to look in the other direction, towards the town, Swift saw that beyond it lay a hill with a church or some kind of monument at its summit. A graveyard perhaps. A crown of trees.

The policemen, meanwhile, had reached the tearooms on the middle platform. Swift wondered if they would have to go inside. He glimpsed a stutter of images from the well-known film that had been shot there. Clipped voices, shades of grey. Cauliflower clouds of soot-flecked steam. Baggy suit trousers, trenchcoat and trilby. Pillbox hat. Tightly fitted skirt. How much he recalled and how much was invention, he couldn't say. But he remembered the music, a piano concerto, richly romantic, full of yearning. Forced separation. Tears, heaving bosoms.

In the end, she – the conflicted heroine at the apex of the film's relationship triangle – had abandoned her lover and stuck by her husband. *You've been a long way away.* Yes. *Thank you for coming back to me.*

Maggie, too, had been a long way away – but had not come back to him.

Cuck-oo, cuck-oo.

Swift had seen the film many times. Before, during and after the break-up of his marriage. Mainly after. In the film, the lover had been terribly, terribly British. Took it on the chin. Terence hadn't needed to. Swift remembered the day he had come home to find Terence in their home, standing there with Maggie, and she had attempted to laugh it off as nothing serious, tossing her tight auburn curls. Terence had stood there in the centre of their living room, with his open-neck shirt and his sports jacket, surrounded by Swift's bookshelves. Smoking some kind of bitter-smelling cigarette. This was their home, Swift remembered thinking, their nest.

Some excuse had been made and Terence had departed, but Maggie had left soon afterwards and, apart from at his father's funeral, when she'd hovered at a distance, Swift had never seen her again.

Swift walked back down the town side of the railway bridge and crossed the car park to re-enter the station. He passed under the tracks by means of the pedestrian tunnel and caught up with the policemen by the site of the poem he had read on his arrival. He politely asked what was going on and one of the officers told him a VIP was expected. He asked them who it was. The policeman exchanged a glance with one of his colleagues, then smiled grimly, adding that he wasn't at liberty to say.

Swift looked at the great station clock as he turned to go. The reading was shortly due to begin. He passed beneath the tracks and traversed the car park. He misjudged the height of the kerb and tripped, his glasses falling off his nose and landing with a sharp snap on the pavement. With difficulty he bent to pick them up. One lens was cracked in two places. He had always preferred glass lenses because they didn't scratch. They broke instead.

He folded the glasses away into his jacket pocket and walked back towards the centre of the town. He felt smaller and everything around him seemed both dangerously close and yet further away. People loomed as they passed him, indistinct yet full of a threatening familiarity. When he reached the crossroads, he took the broken glasses from his pocket and put them on. Straight on, the road continued to climb the hill, past a guest house and on towards the church or monument he had seen from the railway bridge. He felt an attraction, but he knew it was time for his reading. He had never missed a reading, never left a venue while there was still someone waiting to get a book signed.

So he turned right, fumbling his glasses back into his pocket, and half-guessed, half-felt his way past the pub he had been told was there, until he reached the right building. A flight of steps led upwards. He climbed them with difficulty, passing a man in a sports jacket standing on the top step smoking a cigarette.

Once inside, Swift removed his glasses from his pocket and put them on. Right away he could see he had entered via the wrong door. The room was full and the table containing copies of his books was at the far end. Two women stood between the table and another doorway, clearly the one through which he ought to have arrived. While deciding what he should do, he allowed his gaze to settle on the audience.

The room was full, as if the whole town had turned out to hear him read, as if *he* were the VIP whose arrival had been expected.

A ridiculous idea, unless the town were not an ordinary town.

He looked from one face to the next — even in three-quarter profile they could easily be made out — and from one row to the next. His gaze scanned the whole room. Row after row. Face after face after familiar face.

In the front row, by an empty seat, the back of a head, tight shoulder-length curls, still the same shade of auburn with perhaps a little help.

He removed his broken glasses as he turned back to the doorway by which he had come in, his breaths laboured. As he exited the building, he passed someone coming back in trailing a cloud of pungent cigarette smoke. A bitter, heady aroma.

Swift stumbled as he negotiated the steps, but righted himself. Speed was important, he sensed, in case he should be followed.

At the crossroads and traffic lights, he turned right, crossing the road, and started making his slow, painful way up the hill. Away from the town, away from the railway station. As he climbed, he saw them all again, row upon row upon row.

He wanted to stop, needed a rest, but somehow he kept going, dragging his feet up the hill. He pictured the church, the graveyard, the crown of trees. At the top he would rest. In peace.

Above him in the darkening sky, the swifts had fallen silent, but still those tiny black sickles continued to sweep back and forth.

Dinner of the Dead Alumni

Adam Marek

Today the streets of Cambridge are crawling with dead alumni. Their ghosts perch on punts, trailing their fingers through the green weed without raising a ripple. They fly round Trinity College's Great Court, performing the 367m run before even the tenth of the twenty-four chimes. They cheer themselves, but their cheers reach no corporeal ears. The dead waft through the Grand Arcade, raising goosebumps on the fresh navels of girls texting outside Topshop. They hover at the doorway of the Apple store, whooping every time a fresh burst of radio waves casts them across the concourse and dashes their weightless bodies on the ground.

Preston cannot see them, but ever since he and Yolanda arrived with their twin girls, he has been aware of something funky in the air.

Static discharges from the ghosts of Trinity College have horripilated every hair on his body, and it is these upright antennae that have made him as sensitive as a flytrap. This hypersensitivity allows Preston to notice, for the first time, the unearthly magnetism of Kelly from all the way across the Apple store.

Something about Kelly wakes up his belly button. It blinks and blinks as if this is the first girl it has ever seen. Preston knows her name is Kelly because that is what it says on her badge. Her job title though, two point sizes smaller, defies both his eyes and his belly button. To all seeing parts of his body, she is just Kelly, dark curls tumbling at her neck, wearing a helter-skelter of candy stripes. Preston falls all the way down her and leaves his breath at the top.

When she puts down the iPhone and leaves the shop, Preston cannot help but follow.

Yes, Preston is married. Yes, he has twin girls. Here they all are, coming out of the Grand Arcade public toilets, stopping to watch the teenage boy with the bright orange hair run at the wall, bound up its surface, and then flip himself over. The rubber soles of his Converse boots slap the pavement with a sound that knocks olives from ciabattas. Even the ghosts stop to watch the boy. Here is an amazed Bertrand Russell with his arms folded across his chest.

The twins, Libby and Daniela, are lively now they've peed. Their fingers are still wet from washing, pulling at the ties of Yolanda's top, snapping threads, until Yolanda smacks the back of their hands and begs them to leave her alone for just one moment.

The girls have dried ice cream around their mouths. There is something porcine in the flair of their nostrils. These are identical twins. If they were even a little different, they would not draw stares the way they do. Yolanda tries to ignore the people who are so fascinated by her uncanny younglings. She holds their hands high enough to prevent mischief and marches them through the arcade towards the Apple store.

Today, the Master of Trinity College has invoked the memory of the dead. It is 350 years since the college's greatest alumnus, Isaac Newton, first attended the college, and it is 100 years since Ludwig Wittgenstein first came to the campus. A moment in time worthy of marking. Living alumni from around the world have come to Cambridge to celebrate, elbow to elbow with the dead.

In the chapel, delighted tourists startle Newton's statue with their camera flashes. One Vietnamese lady is so excited, she feels herself re-made by Trinity's architecture. Something of its grandeur has straightened her spine. She pokes her enormous glasses hard against her face. Now Cambridge is inside her, proud and worthy. Its lawns lay down for her. This is where she will send the children she has yet to conceive, *if* they don't get into Hogwarts.

All around Cambridge, in halls and houses, blue gowns are pulled over heads. Trinity's wizards group together where they find each other on the streets. A magical fraternity, for whom Wordsworth's 'Loquacious clock' speaks, so special even the sun has got its hat on.

In Trinity College Hall, high up in the rafters, a wooden mallard listens to the sounds of cutlery being placed far below, and to the percussion of crockery rolling like spun pennies at each of the guests' places.

Distracted like this, the duck does not notice AA Milne and Jawaharlal Nehru behind it whispering to each other and giggling. Wondering if, between them, they can conjure enough solidity in their fingertips to break this bird's inertia.

We must feel sorry for this mallard, who has been moved from rafter to rafter by ingenious pranksters for decades. Who has watched bread broken by England's best minds from vertiginous heights, while not one crumb has ever been cast in its direction.

Kelly moves fast in heels, even over cobbles. Preston weaves around the tourists, keeping her candy stripes in sight. To understand why he chases her vapour trail like this, you must know about a girlfriend Preston had when he was 16. She told him something that would haunt him forever.

Her name was Annabel, and she was a violent kisser who left his lips swollen and tender and tasting of cherry Chapstick. He cannot think about her without hearing the sound of incisors clashing. She told him that for every person, there is a partner so perfect that if you touch them, you'll both orgasm immediately.

Preston had many questions about Annabel's myth, such as, would orgasm occur *every* time these two people touched each other? If, say, the magic happened in a train carriage where the two people were standing, and the rocking of the train was knocking them together again and again, would they come repeatedly? Was the effect expendable? Annabel had only a surface knowledge of this phenomenon and was unable to answer his questions.

He and Annabel did not share this magical property. They worked each other sore to reach such climaxes. But this idea stayed with him, fascinated him, throughout his life. The assessment of girls for this property was simple and discreet and he conducted it frequently. Obsessively. He did it in pubs, in queues at the cinema, at the supermarket, never finding her.

His relationships were always short. To him, they could only be temporary because despite their individual merits, what was the point in being with anyone but his absolute perfect match?

It sounded to Preston like a most inconvenient gift, and yet he yearned for it. An orgasm that one did not have to work for, that came unsolicited at some unsuspecting moment, would surely be the most wondrous of all.

Throughout Preston's thirty-two years, he had sloughed the beliefs of his youth, leaving the most outrageous first. He skipped over Santa and crunched fairies and werewolves beneath his boots when he was still wearing size 4s. He stomped on people who could move objects with their minds and did not look back.

But this one belief, in the spontaneous orgasm of two people perfectly attuned to each other, stayed with him. It had been so appealing to his 16-year-old mind, and it was so impossible to disprove by scientific study, that he clung to it. The last piece of magic on Earth. And today, the day that Trinity's dead walk the streets of Cambridge, he feels more certainly than ever before that he has found his orgasmic twin.

Already the blood has rushed from his head into the divining rod which he follows through the market square crowds, past stalls of ostrich meat and novelty Obama t-shirts and Jamaican patties, so enchanted that he ignores the rational part of his mind that reminds him about Yolanda.

Yolanda arrives at the Apple shop. She scans the top of people's heads, because Preston is taller than most men, but he is not there. She moves around the big tables, and pulls the twins' hands away from the laptops, and tells the sales assistants with their weird hair and their informality that she needs no help. Maybe Preston has stooped to look at goodies he cannot afford. She moves through the whole shop twice, and then scans heads again.

Outside the shop, while she takes out her phone and dials Preston's number, Libby and Daniela point amazedly at the ghosts, who are leaning into the wind of radio waves pouring from the shop. The ghosts stretch their arms wide, their eyes closed with delight.

Galumphing down Trinity Street comes the ghost of Aleister Crowley, class of 1898, horny as a dunnock. How desperately he needs something, anything, to make naked magic with. But everywhere he looks, every phantasmic face to which he raises a cheeky eyebrow turns away. Where are all the lady-ghosts? And where are all the adventurous men? These ghosts are shameful in their conventionality.

Aleister bites at the air, bites ineffectually at the necks of the living, until, finally, a pair of luminous eyes meets his – another dead alumnus who has awoken from his sleep engorged, causing Aleister's ectoplasm to bubble.

These ghosts have no need for propriety. The last time either of them loved another like this it was illegal, but watch them now set upon each others mouths with ravenous joy. Fingers groping through layers of refracted light. They drop to the ground, and there, at one thirty on a Saturday afternoon in June, being walked through by students and tourists and terriers, they satiate each other.

Preston is startled by the vibration of his phone in his pocket, and then a second later, the ring begins – the opening beats of Michael Jackson's *Billy Jean*. He takes the phone out, and on the screen is a photo of Yolanda he took last Christmas. She is poking her tongue out.

He lets the phone ring until his voicemail answers, and then he puts it back in his pocket. He will call her in a few minutes once he has decided how to explain that he has to catch up with this girl, lay his hand upon her, to test whether his instincts are correct, that this is the one person on the planet for whom he is specifically made. Surely a demonstration of two people enjoying simultaneous orgasm from one touch alone would negate the need for explanations and excuses? No one bound by mere marital and coincidental attachment could argue with something as miraculous as that.

But now... where is she? From the mouth of Rose Crescent, a tour group in matching purple jumpers has poured into Trinity Street, closing the gaps between bodies through which he was navigating, and despite his height, he has lost her.

Preston tries to push through the people as if he is a ghost, as if he will not bounce off them, but bounce off them he does, and soon, alerted by the angry grunts of people knocked aside, the crowd moves to let him through. To Preston, this almost biblical division of shoppers is another clear sign. The path is so clear that he is able to run, staring into every shop window for a second to see if she has gone inside. Every moment that he does not find her makes it more likely that he will never see her again.

Behind the college, on the river, a raft of punts nods into the weed as each of the students steps upon it. They take hands and help each other onto this buoyant stage, excited because this is the first time they have ever done it. On the banks, students and fellows and parents sit on tartan blankets popping corks and gouging stalks from the hearts of strawberries.

And here too there are ghosts, the angle of the sun turning their blue to gold. They watch the students and ache to feel once more the giddy thrill of an unsteady platform beneath their feet, the simple joy of something that confounds the senses.

Guys in gowns thrust poles deep into the Cam and guide the raft out to the middle. The singers arrange themselves by voice and height as they have rehearsed, and grin because these sensations are still novel.

When they are in position, they wait for a certain stillness that is imperceptible from the bank, and then they open their mouths. The pink bellows that cradle their lungs push out something so sweet it causes champagne pourers to overfill their glasses, and even the dead to weep.

This sound is trampled in the marketplace, where Yolanda kneels before her girls. They have been fighting over Libby's Sea Monkeys keyring – a mini-aquarium the size of a child's fist filled with overfed brine shrimp.

Yolanda holds Daniela's forearm out to show Libby the deep red crescents which fit Libby's fingernails like a glass slipper.

It terrifies Yolanda that they fight like this. When the girls first became aware of each other, before they could even sit up, they would use their chubby little arms like clubs against each other, they would kick with their sticky feet, and they bit before they even had teeth. On their third birthday, Yolanda found Daniela crouched over Libby pressing a cushion onto her face.

Yolanda had suggested to Preston that they take the girls somewhere, to see someone, but he had been adamant that this is how kids behave. Every time the twins fight, Yolanda thinks about the barn owl chicks she saw on *Springwatch*, all hatched a week apart, of different sizes, like Matryoshka dolls, and how they did fit inside one another, because the largest chick ate the others alive. It tipped its head all the way back, shuddering with the effort of swallowing something only one size smaller than itself.

Yolanda calls Preston again, and again gets no answer. Behind her lips, her vitriol is rehearsing.

'Mummy,' Libby says, 'where are all those blue people going?'

'What blue people?' Yolanda says.

And then Libby bolts, her greasy little fingers slipping easily out of Yolanda's hand.

Yolanda yells her name and runs after her as fast as Daniela's feet can keep up, but Libby whips round the knees of people in the market. Yolanda unpacks the voice she only uses at home when the curtains are closed, a full force roar that reconfigures her face and terrifies the shoppers around her. When this sound hits one old dear, she falls into a display of honeydew melons, and they tumble together, bashed knees, bruised melons and a broken wrist. Yolanda picks up Daniela and runs after Libby whose white dress appears only every few seconds as gaps open up between people. Squeezed tight against Yolanda's chest as she runs, Daniela's feet jiggle above the street, whizzing past paper bags and wristwatches. Her chin is knocked by her mother's shoulder and her teeth slam together on her lip. As blood wells up through the split, she starts to howl.

Preston's ankle is throbbing. Weakened by a tennis injury, it cannot cope with these cobbles, but he pushes on. He would run on bloodied stumps if he had to.

Every one of his senses is tuned to the wavelength of red and white candy stripes and he scans the windows of Strada and Heffers and The Royal Bank of Scotland as he charges past. His body flushes with pleasure chemicals as he sees the briefest flash of candy-stripe fabric going through the Great Gate of Trinity College.

On the river, the choir has reached crescendo, their voices threaded together and cast over the bank-side audience, captivating them so deeply that even their breath needs permission.

The sound draws the dead from all over Cambridge. It awakens late risers from their beds – beds which have collapsed around their sleepers, so long have they slept.

The porters wearing their practised faces do not stop porting, but lift up the edges of their bowler hats to trap inside some of the music for later, when they can enjoy it in bare feet, patrolling their rooms with their belts unbuckled.

In the kitchens, the singing is barely audible amongst the sound of wooden spoons in pans, knives on chopping boards, bubbles struggling against glass lids. But it causes the crystal glasses to ring most eerily. It drives the ghost of Byron's bear crazy. Watch it gambol through the dining room, shaking its blue-bloodied muzzle, loping through the completed silver service. Not even the flames atop the candelabra notice it pass.

On the river, the last note pulls behind it a silence so deep and terrifying that every hand feels compelled to fill this void with the most reassuring applause it can muster.

At the Great Gate, Preston queues among the gowned fellows, his extraordinary height allowing him to see over the top of their heads into the Great Court, but his candy-striped girl has vanished.

He lets his phone ring until it tires in his pocket. He still does not have an explanation for Yolanda.

When he looks at his watch, he causes everyone around him to look at their watches, and this need to know the time flows out from him in a great concentric wave, compelling everyone at that very moment to know the time. As if in answer, the clock above the Great Court chimes the hour twice over. It is six o'clock.

At the mouth of the Great Gate, beneath Henry VIII brandishing his wooden chair-leg, Preston notices for the first time that he is the only one in the queue not wearing a gown and the only one not carrying an invitation card.

On King's Parade, everyone stops to look at their watches together, and in this moment of stillness, they stare at Yolanda running. She is an impressive sight, her plaited ponytail slapping at her back. The cords in her neck come out to amplify her voice as she yells Libby's name. Her flip-flops slap the paving, ticking out the double chimes of Trinity's clock. And over her shoulder, Daniela, hypnotised by shaking, clings to her mother's chest, watching the amazed faces recede behind her.

Ahead of them, Libby chases the ghosts.

Now they have all arrived at the college, the living and the dead. The ghosts need no invitation, and melt through the queue like it's not there, melt through Preston, who is shuffling forward in the procession. He watches each person in front showing their invite to the porter. This porter looks like he is immune to bargaining. He has a big-chested solidity and eyes that have no whites. His mouth does not reciprocate smiles.

Preston apologizes as he cuts sideways through the crowd, towards a group of four younger men in gowns. One of them has some kind of colourful juggling equipment, and the others are gathered around him, examining it. Their conversation stops as he approaches, and their mouths open slightly when they appreciate his size. Preston hunches in the way that he does.

'I've forgotten my invite,' he says. 'And my gown. I'll give you two hundred quid for a loan of one of yours.'

'I don't get undressed for less than five hundred,' the juggler-boy says laughing outrageously at himself. 'And I don't think it would fit you anyway.' The laughter of the other boys spills all over the pavement, splashes against Preston who stands as still as a lighthouse, his face ignited. He retreats back into the queue, a full head taller than anyone else.

On the ground, Aleister Crowley's mouth is at the neck of his man, whispering incantations over his neon moles. This couple is insensible of footsteps and the heavy pendulums of carrier bags. Aleister's spell unwraps itself, a mischievous gift, something from the other side, loosening the screws of gravity.

Preston's fantastic height has caught the attention of the porter at the gate. Preston has seen him note the pink collar of his shirt — so alien among the starched-white-on-navy of the fellows' uniforms. Far ahead, through the arches of the fountain, climbing the stone steps to the Hall, is the candy-striped woman. She is now wearing a gown, and the fabric swishes about her, revealing slivers of her wonderful stripes.

Now the queue has narrowed at the mouth of the entrance. There are only three people ahead of Preston. Fear floods his system with something radioactive, something that burns at his joints. Fear of being turned away, and fear of never knowing whether this woman was the one.

The fear turns to energy and energy turns to action. To the amusement of the fellows around him, Preston steps straight over the barrier and runs.

The porter calls out stop. Gives chase. Other porters come. Other men in gowns pursue him. But Preston is a daddy long-legs, each of his strides covering three of a normal man's. He pounds across the lawn, past the fountain. Those behind him cannot keep up, and those ahead of him stand aside for fear of the violent strength such a giant could command.

For the second time today, a path clears for Preston.

He leaps up the stone steps in a single bound, into the corridor, past the ghosts of Newton and John Dryden and Francis Bacon who stand before their portraits imitating their own expressions.

He ducks low through the entrance to the Hall, and two hundred faces all turn towards him.

Trinity Street is awash with gowns and chatter, and in this confusion, Yolanda has lost sight of Libby. She imagines someone, some dribbling, broken-toothed paedophile putting pawprints on her white dress and over her mouth. Faced with this terrifying vision she stops and gathers up everything she has inside her. Her yell is so fierce it moves through the crowd like a shockwave. Ankles, unbolted by Aleister Crowley's tongue, betray their owners. Yolanda's ululation fells everyone. Every knee, every hip, every elbow and every shoulder on Trinity Street, in one great wave hits the pavement. There is a collective groan as the force of the fall pushes air from the lungs of more than three hundred people.

At the end of her scream, Yolanda's teeth sing like a tuning fork.

Before the fallen pick themselves up, while they are too shocked to even apologise to those they have scratched and groped as they fell, the only person standing is Libby, and an orchard of ghosts who stand rooted to the stones, staring at Yolanda. The force of her howl against their backs was a delicious sensation worth all of those numb decades.

Amongst them, Libby is staring at her smashed keyring aquarium, crying.

In the rafters, the mallard watches the colossus step into the room, and is suddenly airborne. Its wings are moulded firmly to its sides and all attempts to flap are futile. It watches the room turn around it, sees far above, its former perch and behind it, AA Milne and Jawaharlal Nehru high-fiving each other in delight. And then it crashes to the ground.

This isn't how Preston wanted this moment to be.

Standing in the middle of Trinity's fellows, ten feet tall and clutching a Waterstones bag, sweaty from the pursuit, he scans the room and finds his girl. The timing of the duck's fall is so precise that there is a common misperception that he has knocked his head against the rafters and dislodged it.

The porters have waited moments while they gathered together in enough numbers to tackle this monster. Eight of them move in on him. Preston sees the girl, sitting on a bench close-by. One leg is crossed over the other, revealing a bare knee so smooth that his gaze can't settle upon it without sliding down her shin.

His insides are a-shiver. Closing the gap between himself and Kelly in two great strides, he takes in all of her. He can imagine the weight of her curls against his face, the plush smothering smack of her lips.

She recoils as he approaches, sliding her bottom along the bench, but already he is there. For the first time he is able to read the rest of her name badge: Dr Kelly Campbell, Dept of Physics.

It will all make sense in a moment, he tries to say, but he is panting and his words come out all mashed into one. He could never have imagined that this moment of revelation, which should be spectacular for them both, would have happened with an audience. But somehow it is fitting.

Preston reaches out and wraps his long fingers around Kelly's wrist. She tries to pull away, and even stands up, but it is too late. The magic is already happening.

The sensation begins simultaneously in Preston's balls and his feet, rocketing through his insides, hormonal fireworks fizzing against the underside of muscles and curling round bones, making his titanic cartilage groan with pleasure.

He is compelled to close his eyes, to fully savour the fanfare that is boiling in his underpants, but he does not. Something is wrong.

Kelly is still trying to wrestle free from his grip. Her face shows no sign of supernatural ecstasy. Only horror.

Preston is coming alone.

It is too late to stop. Even if he let go of her now. His insides are on fire and the fire will not stop until he is all ashes. He has never felt an orgasm like this before. Hidden fuses throughout his systems flare and blow. Cells chime against cells. The pleasure is uncontainable, and his terror makes it even sweeter. Terror because now he sees all around him the blue faces of Trinity's past. Lights obscure his vision. His knees crumple. He is unmade.

Even knelt like this before Kelly, he is still taller than her. And her expression is one of revulsion.

Porters have his collar, have his arms, grab his fingers and force them to relinquish Kelly. Yank him backwards with such velocity he is forced to run on his heels. Men and women gather round Kelly, healing her with their murmurs, and block her from Preston's view.

As the orgasm, the most tremendous orgasm in the universe, subsides, a sense of abjection washes in to fill the space it has left.

The porters drag Preston down the stone steps, across the lawn, to the front gate where queuing fellows still wait. For the third time today, the crowd divides to allow him through.

When Yolanda reaches Libby, the shoppers have stood up and are brushing themselves down, looking around to see what has happened. Maybe they suspect a bomb has gone off. But as soon as the first person has resumed shopping, the others follow, and within seconds, it's as if Yolanda's utterance never existed.

Libby is on her knees, sobbing, picking up the fractured pieces of her Sea Monkeys keyring from the ground. In between cobbles, the little brine shrimp twitch their tails, their segmented legs working the meniscus of their spilled environment.

Yolanda sets Daniela down on the ground. And now that the adrenaline is retreating back into the caves of her body, she feels all the muscles she has pulled in her pursuit. Something holding her spine straight has snapped. Something in her thigh is burning. She is conceiving Libby's punishment when among the crowd of strangers she sees Preston. His walk is weird and hobbled.

'I'm sorry,' he says.

Yolanda starts in with the where-have-you-beens and I've been going crazy I've just had to chase our daughter through the street do you have any idea what... and then she stops because Preston is wearing a familiar expression which she can't quite place.

'I don't feel so good,' he says.

'Why are you walking funny? What the hell happened to you?'

Preston needs time to concoct an explanation. 'I'm okay,' he says. 'Let's just go home.'

But this is not acceptable to Yolanda, and she shifts tack on the questions and suggests scenarios to Preston to which he must reply yes or no. 'Have you been attacked? Have you had an aneurysm?' This method of elimination is unlikely to reveal the exact circumstances that have led Preston to be standing here, concealing a sticky patch of semen from the world with a carrier bag, but Yolanda is relentless.

In the Hall, Preston's fingerprints have faded from Kelly's arm. The mallard has been set upon the head table beside a basket of rolls. The gravy is thickening in the pot. The singers are back on the bank. Byron's bear is cavorting unseen in the river. Aleister and his mate lie on their backs looking up through the people at the blushing sky. They are breathless. The Master of Trinity tings his glass three times with a teaspoon. This dinner of the dead alumni has begun most memorably.

Gifts

Jo Lloyd

The day arrived, inauspiciously, poking its skinny fingers at Mal's eyes. He'd been out on the piss with his dad the night before, taking stick, as usual, from all his dad's mates. Liberace, Mantovani, Richard Clayderman, they'd called him. Forgot your sequins, have you? they'd said, they always said, it was always funny. Fuck off, he'd said, not laughing. He'd matched them pint for pint, despite the recently reiterated threats from his teacher, and even though, with no jobs since Carousel the month before, he'd had to depend on his dad's charity for the beer.

He took two aspirin, had a cigarette for breakfast, then shut himself in the room that used to be the front parlour before the piano was wedged in there like an angular black hole. There was a passage in the new sonata that he was struggling to get his fingers around. He was worried, somewhere so deep that he couldn't name the insect nibble inside him, that he would never get his fingers around it. Above him, his aunty, just out of hospital, kept hammering at her floor, his ceiling, with her cane. Mal must have gone up five times to see what she wanted. Clumsy old cow, he muttered under his breath. I've got the best seat in the house, she said to him. Then later, You certainly can play loud, love. Piss off, he muttered.

When his mam got back from work, he walked into Ponty to get the bus, but at the last minute looked in his wallet and decided to hitch. He got a lift with a thin-haired fat man who sold brushes door-to-door and who spent the whole trip trying to convert him to the good life, the mysteries of carpet brushes and clothes brushes, bristles, synthetic fibres, bonding materials. The doors that could be knocked on, the brush needs that could be fulfilled.

Mal stared out of the window and wished the bloke smoked, at least that would shut his bloody gob. He thought about Bry.

Bry slept late, rehearsing, in her dreams, the effort of waking. The night before she'd got a lift home with Den Richards, who'd wanted to keep on talking until the weight of the universe, settled unaccountably on his shoulders, could be somehow levered off and toppled to the ground. She'd yawned and fidgeted, but she'd let him go on, because she would continue to need rides from him and the other old men who gathered at the bar, night after night, trusting, in the face of all evidence, that their lives could change or find meaning there.

Accustomed to good things being dropped into her lap, Bry didn't realize that she'd been lucky to get this job, nor that her days in it were numbered. She rolled her eyes at the customers' jokes. She piled the glasses in the sink. She spoke tartly or not at all. Mrs Morris would let her go as soon as she could find a pretty girl who didn't think herself too good to smile.

Bry ate toast and jam in the kitchen, several pieces, dropping the crumbs in a book. Her gran came in and lost her temper because that was the last of the bread, and Bry had to listen to another lecture about lying around like lady muck thinking the world owed her a living, before she was sent down to the shop to buy more bread, plus milk of magnesia for her gran's anxious stomach, gnawing, unsated, as so often, on Bry's feckless nature and bleak prospects. In a surge of chalk-induced resolution, her gran insisted she clean her room. No one could plan their future among the drifts of books and photos and god only knew what that swirled around Bry's room in the wake of all the ideas she had gone chasing after and got bored with. Bry sighed loudly and started to sift the flotsam into temporary islands. She thought about leaving.

Mal waited near the bus shelter where the salesman had dropped him. He sat on the grassy slope below the road and smoked, flicking ash moodily at the sheep, who stared at him, jaws churning slowly, as if they were planning their next move. He worked on the development section in his mind, trying out a new fingering. He hoped Bry would be in a better mood today.

Bry came running up from behind and slithered down next to him, bringing with her, as always, a rush of energy that blew away the pins and tacks and nails keeping the world battened down, and sent it all out into space, all the fridges and clocks and floorboards and hoovers and people, tumbling away, so that all that was left was him and Bry, the island of dry grass they were sitting on, the sun beating down, and the sea, far below them, shimmering, a pale blue moonscape that their feet could mark, indelibly, as they walked out across it.

They hadn't seen each other in four days. They made small animal sounds, wrapped around each other, finding a place for all their hands.

Then Bry pulled away. 'Not here,' she said.

He looked around. There were some thistles, a seesaw, a litterbin. 'Is your gran in?'

'Yeah. She's in one of her moods.'

Mal put his arm round her, pulled her close. 'No one's looking,' he said.

'How'd you get here?' she said after a while.

Hitched. He laughed. 'You should of seen this bloke I got a lift with. Right saddo. Drives round the country selling brushes.'

'Sounds alright to me,' said Bry. 'No one telling you what to do.'

'You're joking aren't you? I wouldn't be a salesman if you paid me a million pounds.'

'I'd do anything for a million pounds.'

'Bet you wouldn't.'

'Bet I would.'

Something was prickling in the space between them. Mal's headache, Bry's tiredness, the quarrel they had started four days ago, the invisible future, the big unanswered questions.

He looked at the sea, frowning. 'What shall we do then?'

This was not where either of them had expected to be at this point in their lives.

Mal should have been in music college by now. He'd been working towards it for years. Years of scales and arpeggios and four-part harmony, Czerny and Bach and Chopin, getting up in the dark to practise, learning scores in the backs of buses. He'd gone up to London for the scholarship auditions and found himself suddenly weak, sweating, stupid, as glandular fever, bartered casually off some sharp-faced blonde whose name he couldn't even remember, swept in through a logjam of late nights and hangovers.

He couldn't throw off the virus. His mam said it wouldn't hurt to wait a year. His dad said nothing. He saw them looking past him at the sacrifices going by on a conveyor belt like prizes they hadn't won, music books, teachers, buses, trains. The piano. All shuddering away into the darkness.

He blundered about for a while, got barred from a couple of pubs, was picked up once by the police. Finally his teacher gave him an ultimatum. He was to stop drinking, get his strength back, stay out of trouble. He watched trumpeters and cellists going off to Manchester, Leeds, London. The ground was starting to move, like the swell under a pier. At night, the words of examiners and judges beat in his head. Rushed the scherzo. Inconsistent attack. Tentative cantabile.

Right now, the only sure good thing in his life was Bry. Being with Bry, in bus shelters and pubs and private buzzing glades in the bracken, and just occasionally and best of all, at her house when her gran wasn't there. But he didn't know how long Bry would stay.

Bry should have been at university, but had failed her A Levels so badly she would not even contemplate resitting. Her teachers had warned her. Put the work in now, they had said. It'll be worth it. And she had tried. She had bought ring binders, written essay plans and revision timetables, borrowed extra books from the library. But she had got distracted.

For a long time, she had kept herself out of the parade that took up so much of her classmates' energy. She had seen, in her own family, the warnings. Sex was a trial by ordeal, it left women broken, burnt, drowned. Teenagers fumbling in the back of a car or behind the canteen would barely remember the miserable experience except for the inevitable arrival, nine months later, of a vengeful howling infant.

So when it happened, not in the back of a car because no one at school had a car, and not behind the canteen, where the dinner ladies sighed over their heavy legs, but in Kev Pritchard's house one Wednesday afternoon during double games, it took her by surprise. Not Kev himself, although he turned out to be unexpectedly capable and inventive. What caught her attention, what required her concentrated study over the days that followed, was a shift in the order of things. Time and the fortuitous placement of her features had granted Bry a warrant. It got her out of detentions and into nightclubs, broke the ice at interviews, opened an unobstructed path along pavements, and above all, provided a steady supply of young men eager to confirm her place in the universe.

Then she met Mal. He was handsome enough, although a little shorter than she liked, talented, but not particularly bright, no more special than anyone else, she thought, until one day she found herself looking at his articulate fingers, his long lashes, at the dark eyes dropped carelessly by an Italian immigrant a generation or two before, and quite unable to go on another minute without touching him.

The tide was hurrying out, leaving fresh new streams and rivers chasing the escaping mass of the sea. Mal jumped them, trying to keep his shoes dry. 'Fucking hell,' he said, when water splashed the suede. Bry rolled her eyes. She had no patience with any kind of nicety about waves or weather or footwear.

They walked along, through a scattering of dogs and disconsolate toddlers, then clambered up the slumped cliffs to the path above. They headed to a bench set back in the gorse, where old people wrapped in too many layers for the season could keep out of the cold and count the miles to the horizon.

Mal lit a Regal. Bry looked at the small figures trailing along the beach below. 'I can't wait til we're in London,' she said.

This was the plan. When he went to London she'd go with him. There would be plenty of opportunities there. Art, films, photography. She had decided that it would be nice to be a photographer. You didn't need a degree. You could go where you wanted. Paris, Italy, Bolivia. Or maybe an actress.

'There'll be so much to do,' she said.

'Yeah,' said Mal. He'd taken seventy quid up to London for the auditions. He'd come back with four. He'd gone to La Boheme one night, to the Festival Hall another. He'd gone round Piccadilly with a Scottish lad he'd met at the college and had drunk a lot, despite and because of the glandular fever. He'd had a good time. Even so, he couldn't really account for where the money had gone.

Mal looked at her. 'You know,' he said, a slight vibrato, despite himself, in his voice, 'I didn't mean what I said the other day.'

'No, or I wouldn't be here,' she said.

'I don't like talking about that stuff.'

'I know,' she said, more gently, and she leaned closer, straightened a lock of his hair where it lay on his neck.

'I got you something,' he said.

She smiled. 'You didn't have to.'

'I saw this,' he said, pulling a postcard out of his bag. 'And it just, you know, says, I mean, what I think.'

On the back, in his loose round handwriting, it said Mal XOX. She turned it over. There was no picture, just words printed across the front. 'I love you so much I can't shit.'

She looked at him. 'That's disgusting.'

'It's funny,' he said. He giggled, pleased with himself. 'Don't you think it's funny?'

'No.'

'If you don't think that's funny you got no sense of humour.' He stopped laughing.

She thought of Kev Pritchard looking at her in the dusk of his parents' bedroom. Boys who'd told her she was beautiful. The man on the train who'd said he'd like to paint her.

'Thank you,' she said.

'I suppose you'd prefer some bloody poem,' Mal said.

'I said thank you didn't I?'

They both stared at the sea and the reefs slowly being uncovered by the tide.

'Do you think your gran'll have gone out?'

'I told you, she's not going out.'

A crow came hopping across the grass, tilted its black head at them. Mal threw a pebble at it.

'Mal,' said Bry.

'Fucking things,' he said. 'I hate them. My granddad told me they peck the eyes out of lambs. And worse. Peck at their arses. Pull out their guts.'

'I don't believe that,' she said.

The crow landed a little way off and Mal threw another pebble.

They continued to sit. Mal complained about his aunty and Beethoven. Bry tapped her feet. The day frittered and then it was gone and they were no closer to answering the big questions or even the smaller ones.

'Let's go to the pub,' Bry said.

'I'm skint,' he said.

'I just got paid.'

'I got some bloody pride you know.'

'For god's sake. You can pay next time.'

They climbed up the hill to the pub. They sat outside drinking until it got too cold then they went in and drank some more. Mal started talking about opera. 'It's my favourite musical form after piano,' he said. Bry made a face. 'My bloody favourite,' he said. He started a one-sided debate, getting intense and heated. So heated he swung an elbow into the beer of the man next to him.

'Watch it you fucking idiot,' said the man.

'Who are you calling a fucking idiot you fucking ponce?' said Mal.

They got up, touched chests, brought their faces together, close enough to spit, close enough to kiss. Bry got up too and did a little dance, patting the air down. It didn't distract them. The bloke was seven feet tall, solid as a cliff. 'You fucking poof,' he said. Mal stepped back and hit him as hard as he could.

Gravity was on Mal's side. The big man had drunk ten pints, they were sloshing around in the lower half of him like ballast. When he swung his fist, he rocked in place, missing Mal by several inches.

Before he could try again the landlord was there, herding Mal and Bry out, telling them not to come back. 'Who'd want to fucking come back,' shouted Mal. Bry started marching toward home. Mal ran after her and grabbed her arm and said he was sorry and she was the only thing he cared about. She shook him off and told him to grow up and left him there. Mal had to wait a long time for a lift and got back very late and more than half aware, through the fuddle and the haze, that he'd done something very stupid. The next day at the hospital, holding it to him gently like a stillborn puppy, as if that could make a difference now, he found out he'd broken two bones in his hand.

Things changed quickly after that. Mal skipped his next lesson. His teacher rang to tell him he was an ungrateful imbecile. Mal and Bry bickered, on the phone and when they met. Bry got in the back of a car with someone she met at the pub. It didn't count if Mal didn't see it. Mal took her to a party and Bry got so drunk she could hardly stand. There was a lad saying things of such flattery that she wasn't entirely surprised to find herself going into another room with him, any more than she was to find herself lying, later, on the spinning floor.

That was the last time she saw Mal, a watery figure who loomed up over her and said something angry, then disappeared. They exchanged a couple of short, rude letters, where they said what they thought, but not what they wanted. Bry put the phone down when he rang.

Bry went to London on her own. She visited a couple of galleries, went to the theatre once, a cheap seat behind a column. She did bar work while she waited for serendipity to introduce itself. She progressed through more expensive bars, more exclusive clienteles. She tolerated the compliments of old men too glassy-eyed and short of breath to mind her lack of interest. She laughed at them later with pale young men who offered her pills and powders, stole from her purse when she was unconscious. The price of unconsciousness rose every year. It got more difficult to find work. She got thin. Her face hardened and set. She became invisible, people bumped into her in the street and swore. She lost another job, moved to the north with a man she'd known a week, stayed on when he left, in a little caravan on a patch of muddy ground, with some weepy-eyed cats that turned up looking for food. The neighbours had meetings, devised plans to evict her, but finally it was just too difficult and they allowed her to stay. She fed the cats and herself when she remembered. She spent a lot of her time sitting on the caravan steps, staring out, over the damp scrubby fields, toward what she knew must be the horizon.

When Mal's hand healed, he started playing again, but it wasn't the same. He entered a couple of competitions but didn't even get staged. For a while, he picked up enough jobs to keep him going, a musical here or there, some accompanying. Then it dried up. He went into his dad's building business. He filled out, slowed down, had four children by three different women. His hair thinned. He complained about his ex-wives to anyone who would listen. He got the odd chest pain, cut down to half a pack a day. He wouldn't pay for his kids to take music, said he didn't want that pressure on them. For a long time, without telling anyone, he would go by himself to the opera. Then he stopped. Every so often, at a wedding or a party, he'd be talked into playing, and everyone would marvel at how his fingers moved across the keys. At the way the bass notes boomed, rich and solid as the sea in a cave. At how the melody sang out, sweet and pure and unearthly, as if a glimpse had been granted, for just a few moments, through the cold barred gates of heaven.

Losing My Religion

Alison Napier

My name is Victoria. That is all you need to know. Victoria. Named after an aunt who kept a shoe shop in Fife. Running a shoe shop by herself until she died, trying to retire when she reached seventy but no one wanted to buy a shoe shop in a village that got bypassed when the main road came, so she had a closing down sale which lasted six years and some of the stock went but then she died. Leaving a back room full of footwear that had gone stratospherically out of fashion and a shop window obliterated with a poster proclaiming SALE! For years she gave me shoelaces and insoles and shoehorns made from antlers every time she saw me. Sometimes I bought a pair of slippers to help her. Old lady tartan boot-slippers with wispy pom poms, or brown leather men's ones that were always too big, the kind you beat a child with. I shuffled round my flat polishing the lino.

And now things are like this:
      We pushed our way through a lurching group of young men to a table against the wall. It was dark. 'Atmospheric', suggested Companion. 'It's dark', I said. Doubly dark because we were in the sealed sun-free tomb that is an international airport and it was five fifty in the morning. One of the men had swaying furry antlers on his head and they were all slopping pints of lager. The stag staggered and his male mates guffawed.
      I shoved my way through them again to the bar and ordered two full English breakfasts. Companion was pulling books down from a shelf and showing me pictures of exotic crockery and textiles. 'Look', she said when I got back, 'isn't that beautiful?' I glanced at the images of seventh century

pottery and squinted at my watch. The drunk men weaved past in a Bambi samba and people looked away.

A waiter in a long navy Parisian apron appeared with two huge plates of fried food. I buttered toast and shovelled scrambled eggs and sausages into my face. I checked my watch again. Six ten in the morning. Beyond the restaurant, open to the concourse, it was bright and busy under unnatural lights. Unintelligible tannoys droned over the hum of humanity on the move. Unattended luggage. Check-ins opening. Proceed to gates. Suspicious packages. Six fifteen.

We are outside the restaurant now, looking around for routes to our flight, discussing the purchase of a sandwich for later. Unattended luggage. Security. Passengers Robinson and Blanc proceed immediately to. The name is familiar, the name is mine, the future was bright and I am about to miss my flight because I was eating bacon and triangular processed potatoes proceed immediately to Gate Six where flight BE643 is preparing to depart. Jesus wept, run rabbit run, but the sandwich, the newspaper, RUN so I ran and whimpered and ran and ran and got lost and shouted at a man in a fluorescent jacket WHERE IS GATE SIX and he pointed, startled, and I ran down another sloping carpeted corridor as tannoys echoed again and I skidded to a halt and showed my passport and was the last on the plane and now I know that planes are not like buses that will wait if they see you puffing up to the stop. I groped to a seat, blinking tears of rage at myself as they slammed the door, the flight crew did their post-crash drama and I strapped myself in and kicked my bag under the seat. Hard to believe but I am what I think they call a frequent flower. I am subliminally postponing again what I am sure will be my certain death one more time.

The Boeing nine nine nine (which service please) rumbled along a runway, paused, roared into an inferno of life and rushed us headlong into the blue.

But first, introductions. I am Victoria Robinson. The companion is not important. I shall call her Absentia Blanc. We are heading for somewhere foreign that we booked at a time when we liked each other. About nine months ago. Does this happen to other people?

We went up, thrilled and excited, stayed high for a long time and then gradually without even noticing beyond a strange sensation in the chest (the bit where tears hibernate) went down and down into clouds and turbulence and came to a shuddering halt in a barren and alien landscape.

The plane landed, and we queued for this and that, smiling with uncomprehending anxiety. We followed other people and they followed us and we all got onto a shuttle bus for the ten white-knuckles ninety-minute ride into the city. We ate a sandwich in secret, surreptitiously breaking bits off. We looked out of opposite windows and I saw building works and abandoned machinery, diggers and cranes, and I saw lopsided corrugated rusty iron shanty hamlets and mournful long-eared sheep staring exhausted into the middle distance, or do I project, I do not know what Absentia saw and the bus raced on, lurching between lanes as the driver lit cigarettes and looked anywhere but at the road, finally flinging itself over the bridge across the Bosphorus.

I stepped trembling off the bus, and waited for my suitcase. Taxi drivers appeared, locusts swarming, yellow cars placing the bus under siege, all of us hostages to fortune. 'Taxi – you need taxi', an order not a question, and strong arms effortlessly tossed cases and rucksacks into already open car boots, defying owners not to follow, and so in this spectacularly un-British way did I arrive at our city centre apartment.

We found it (nine months ago – did I say?) on an internet site buried deep in the pistons of a search engine. It was cheap, at the top of a five-storey block without a lift in an unfashionable and poor residential area of Istanbul. It was perfect. Even our self-selected taxi man could not find the address without asking many baffled pedestrians. We have barely spoken, Absentia and I. We are here for two weeks.

I have brought my binoculars so that I can watch people without having to get close enough to talk to them. This is the equivalent of wearing sunglasses all the time. Or maybe a veil. I have also brought a headscarf with me for wearing in the mosques. I practise wearing it like the Queen when she is on a drizzly visit to a civic opening in

Huddersfield. I try the chemo style, tied bravely at the back of the neck.

The apartment has a tiny balcony and this, with the price, is why I chose it over other more salubrious locations. It is an eyrie perched above a narrow cobbled street, a street that ends in crumbling-away steps on which small brown boys play with a football. This is why the taxi man had to reverse crossly all the way back. Tell me about it.

So. What I did on my holidays? And the call to prayer ricochets round the city, a fervent Chinese whisper that gets louder and louder. For the love of God.

Absentia has got religion, but not this one. A different one but also from the East. Boo. That woke you up. Boo. Who? Don't make me laugh.

We have a statue of Boohoo in our garden. No. We had a house but we don't have a house now so we don't have a garden so Boohoo is in the rented property don't ask so boring. I cried me a river boo hoo, I had a house I lost a house they stole my heart away dotcom. I had insurance to cover every other unfortunate incident in my life (broken car, sick pet, stolen property, income protection) but no policy even on day time TV with elderly retired sitcom actresses offered to cover me for this. Details don't matter but there they are anyway. Does this happen to other people too?

The teacher's apartment was small with a rotting smell in the bathroom and illegal electrics. The double mattress sagged sorrowfully and was shrouded in a grey mosquito net like city smog. The naked duvet had rimmed stains, and some stuffing poked out through a black and scorched gaping hole over which had been clumsily sewn part of a pillowcase. The patch was coming off, as patches invariably will.

I imagined a couple of beautiful people, propped up on pillows in the afternoon, afterwards, sighing smugly, one leaning across the other for Marlboros and matches, stretching, a nipple almost within mouth's reach again, flicking the soft pack, lighting one and passing it over, lighting the other, leaning back, a flat aluminium ashtray with three pencil-thick dents propped between them on raised knees on the duvet, as you do, free hands on the other's naked thigh, stroking, murmuring, inching even closer, turning to each other with a *mmmm I'm lovin' it* as they prop the cigarettes in the ashtray. An open mouth bends down to find what it missed, stays awhile, comes back up for air, legs rearrange themselves, the cigarettes tip off the ashtray and Whoosh it's all gone up in smoke! And there is none without fire as we know and so they spring apart, caught, laughing in fear, hopelessly fanning the flames with a pillow, leap out of bed and one runs to the kitchen for a basin of water but it was a small fire after all, it is out, all passion spent, pull on tee shirts and jeans and lean against the door frame, deflated, to survey the damage.

Absentia left me for another or so I thought or so she said, I think. Does this happen?

Here are some lies. We were made for each other. We lived happily ever after. We knew each other like we knew ourselves. We were each other's other half. We spent long lazy afternoons smoking afterwards in bed. Fire in the belly. Something struck me. It was a match made in heaven.

Here are some Frequently Asked Questions. What's love got to do with it? Where do you go to my lovely? Is this the way to Amarillo?

I switch on my camera. Memory Full. And also my hard-drive SIM-card head, I thought. No space left. Delete some of your favourites to make room. I deleted my favourite. In my crazy head I sailed to Madagascar. Forgive me.

I sailed to Madagascar and my heart burst open like a seedpod on a South Pacific shore. Atriums and ventricles showered joy, silverpink with shimmering proud mothers of pearls, and I was dusted with golden sparkling sands while tropical insects hummed contentedly when I sailed to Madagascar.

'And then what happened?' the old man asked as he rocked back and forth on his mahogany chair.

'And then what happened?' That goes in the lie bit too. Did I say?

Absentia, obscured by the billowing smoke or so it seemed of a conflagration of bed linen, packed a modest suitcase she had once retrieved from the municipal tip whilst depositing a few redundant domestic items, thus demonstrating once more her inability to grasp the most simple of social conventions, giving with one hand and taking with the other, and leapt into a taxi and headed for the station. Or so she said.

'I need to get away', she said.

'Boo hoo poor you', I said.

Sometimes I am not very nice to those whom I profess to love and cherish. But I get what I deserve and I give as good as I get because surely it is better to give than to receive. My own grasp on things is also not what it might be. The rules of the game have confused me since birth.

'But we've booked a holiday!' I wailed.

In another part of my fractured life, hard to imagine, I had a job and a password for a computer. My password was her name and age. After a year the computer urged me to change it so I changed it to Absentia and the date she left me. Confirm password? OK.

I wailed but she had already gone. Perhaps she sailed to Madagascar or got the train to Edinburgh. I wailed and took to my bed with six detective novels and a box of Cabernet Sauvignon. I read and tried to solve the mysteries ahead of the chief inspectors but I was baffled and bruised and I missed all the clues and soon the words swam and the sentences shifted like fault lines and the light faded and an owl called from deep in the fir-tree forest and I knew there would not be a happy ending with so many careless missing-in-action lives and false alibis.

So here is another lie. I am in an apartment in Istanbul and I am alone. There was only one breakfast in the airport restaurant and only one name called by the tannoy police, only one lunatic lunge through a pressure-sealed door. I lied, I lied. Pants on fire.

The balcony is narrow and the parapet is fractionally too low for the timid and the risk-averse. I lean over it and play at being startled, by a swooping bird perhaps or an exhaust backfiring, and imagine tumbling forward. This makes my stomach heave and I use this test to confirm my status as a sentient being.

I dry pools of rain left over from the overnight shower off the white plastic armchairs. There are two. I sit on one and put my feet up on the other. Alone in Istanbul.

A crackle of static from the minaret opposite signals the next call to prayer. All the elegant spires that I spy with my binoculars on my balcony horizon sweep are joining in, discordant and jarring, hypnotic and atonal, Gregorian and Taizé chanting, echoing, pausing for effect and for breath and then fading one by one until only one remains, the last brave sentinel in the skies. The city sounds reassert themselves, sirens and taxi horns, the hoot of ferryboats on the river, the calls of the street sellers. Who might dare resist such an impassioned call for reverence? Me. Me.

*

Back when we were happy, oh happy day, we lived together in a remote and storm-drenched rough and ready dwelling high on a windswept wasteland. We disposed of other insignificant people as humanely as possible before choosing each other as our future significant other.

My, doesn't that sound grand? Doesn't that sound like something from an interview in a colour Sunday magazine with a distinguished novelist describing how he met his latest wife? 'She was married to my best friend at the time, but we knew straightaway that we had to be together. People got hurt and we deeply regret that, of course. But if we cannot follow our hearts then what is left? Love does not take no for an answer. Shakespeare puts it very well in…' The interviewer is in awe of such arrogance. The photograph shows the happy couple, minus the casualties, standing shoulder to shoulder with a chocolate brown Labrador at their feet for they are too old to start another family, and god knows there are enough families to go round already, in their lovely shiny converted farm house in the Dordogne. God knows.

So no, we were not like that.

A little background. She loved me and then she stopped. That's the background.

The static is crackling again. Perhaps I should stand up. I stand up.

This morning I woke at quarter to five again. I was sleeping under a thin cotton quilt cover but with the burnt duvet at the ready in case it got cold. The cover had Bart Simpson on it, grinning under his vertical yellow chef's hat hair. I was alone. Alone in an apartment in the area known as Beyoglu, a stones throw from the ferry at Kasimpa□ a on the northern side of the Golden Horn in a city of over eleven million souls, I did not learn how to pronounce the names and I can only count up to five.

Out on the balcony again as the sun rises and the prayings swirl around like highland mist, I sit on the damp plastic feeling a chill seeping into the back of my legs. I have a thin wool blanket over my knees; I am disguised as a crone. My hands are clasped piously under my chin but instead of hope or straws they clutch a mug of tea. I sway in time to the music and wish it would never end. I crane forward, looking across my cityscape.

There has been a shower of satellite dishes in the recent past and they landed, perfectly formed snowflakes, on all the rooftops from here to the horizon. The far away ones are tidy, compact discs resting in clumps like mushrooms that have sprouted on damp tile-red carpets. Sometimes they are solitary, one on a chimneystack here, one on a pebble-dashed wall there. But here in the narrow streets full of apartment blocks and narrow hotels and random bits of half-built houses and old wooden shops selling water and potatoes and cigarettes and loose tea, in the clutter and chaos of just across the street the roof tops are a child's playgroup picture, there are no tidy lines, no set square right angles, buildings are turned instead towards each other like therapists and clients, roofs are crumbling away or so it seems, the builders losing interest as they reach the upper floors, slinging tiles side by side over the top level that is open anyway so that the women can hang out the washing even if it is wet, the tiles slipping away, fading out like a sentence that was not worth bothering to end, the meaning long since evaporated in a shrug of disinterest. And onto these abandoned rooftops a man has climbed at great risk to his safety and he has flung a handful of sloppy cement onto the ridge such as it is and he has stuck a metal post with a satellite dish on it and the cement has set in grey lumps and there it is – a south-facing dish from which to serve up the soup of entertainment that bounces round the skies, dodging prayers.

I look through the binoculars and read their imaginatively poetically coupled names. Vestel and Atomsav. Next and Nexstar. Arcelik and Beko. Choose me.

I watch the satellite dishes because I do not have a television set. At the end of the street there is a gap where a house fell down so the owner may have scratched his head for a moment then barrowed in some chicken wire and bits of wood and now in the space there are seven white hens with huge yellow feet stepping daintily over rubble and they join in with the daily cacophony and squawk indignantly, in unison, in the early morning dawn as they blink in the light and fall off their perches.

But I cannot hide on a balcony reading a guidebook, however good the pictures are of temples and mosques and palaces and bustling streets. A whole section is devoted to the food of this city and I stare at the rich pastries oozing honey, and the glistening skewered peppers and aubergines, and the deep fried triangles of crisp filo bursting with cheese. I have been eating salami sandwiches for six days now because I went to the supermarket only once after dark and saw bread and cold meat and tomatoes and dried apricots and that is what I bought. I looked frantically for wine but could see none and did not know the word and did not want to cause offence or to draw attention to my desperation.

But suddenly it is clear. Twenty twenty. I will take a trip. The guidebook recommends an excursion to the Islands. I will go to the Islands. Quick before you change your mind!

The weather is improving for it was not overcast; it was simply that the sun had not yet risen. When will I learn to give situations a chance to develop and improve before I write them off.

And did I go? I went! I crammed a jumper and the guide book and all my money into my bag, along with some dried apricots and water, and slung the binoculars across my chest like a bus conductor, remembered the keys (for that is a drama I would not handle well) and left the apartment. Left the apartment!

Whoosh in a dervish swirl I am down the stairs and there are eighty four of them because I counted them when I came back from the supermarket, and I am already out of breath but I pause at the bottom only for a second and push the wrought iron front door and I am on the street. It is narrow, and the pavement is unusually high, but I stride out as if I know what I am doing. Head for the ferryboats I tell myself for I did not check either the location of my transport or the times of their departures. But fate must beam down on such a commendable and spontaneous plan and so I keep my nerve.

On and on, in a straight line for I have learnt about this city through my binoculars, up and down, dodging the bread sellers with their bagel-snacks and across a busy main street where a tram rings its bell and misses me by inches and on and on and all around the Galata Watchtower and down again past cafes and musical instrument shops and clothes shops and stray cats and dogs and bookshops and down here at street level the call to prayer starts again and I can hardly hear it because I am not in my minaret any more. Fear spreads over me like a blush.

I race across the final road between me and the ferry terminal and the yellow taxis slow and toot, not for my safety but in case I am their next fare, and suddenly I am jabbering at a man behind a grill in a kiosk, I am offering my confession, I am buying a ticket, pointing to my book, giving a hundred Turkish lira and hoping for change as I can only count to five and do not have a clue. Young men thrust leaflets into my hand, 'Eat here, my restaurant, good food, ten percent discount!' I take them all and push through a turnstile and am waved onto a ferryboat and I am aboard. It worked.

But all the adrenaline drains away as the men on the quay shout to each other and thick ropes are unwound from bollards and the water is churned white as we start to reverse and I have found a seat outside, a wooden bench, in a corner, but I do not want to be here, there are unleashed children racing up and down and couples with their arms round each other and sun glasses and unwise tans and I slump deeper into my corner and wonder what possessed me to leave the safety of my beloved, my beloved balcony. I close my eyes and shudder.

The sun is high now in the sky and I feel it burning my face as we turn and head into the Sea of Marmara. I rest my hand against my cheek; it is damp with tears again. With my other hand I ease the palm away, nurse it in my lap and let the late summer heat dry my eyes. I can sit rocking back and forward, whimpering, any day, and I must not do it here. I straighten up, accept a plastic cup of tea from a waiter and turn back to my guidebook.

Kinaliada, Heybeliada, B☐ y☐ kada, Burgazada and Sedefada. I whisper the names and make them a prayer to the gods of all islands everywhere.

B☐ y☐ kada won the public vote and we all jostled off onto the quaint quay in a disorganised crowd. I am learning to be alone. The sun beat down on my scarfless head and I set off to walk to the monastery on the hill. The streets were lined with the summer homes of the rich and maybe famous, huge and beautiful wooden mansions with gardens overflowing with pines and hibiscus, frontages facing the sea, oh to live in a happy palace. I would wake in the day light and reach out to touch you, reach out to know you were there, reach out I'll be there, I would be an outreach worker.

I did not know that you would go.

I stumbled on, up through wide tree-lined streets; I was out of breath and out of time. The last quarter of a mile was steeper, designed for pilgrims and donkeys. The crowds have thinned, everyone is quiet now, wiping sweat from faces, stopping for breath on the pretext of admiring the crazy blue sea on all sides. Suddenly a little boy comes hurtling downwards, fearless on the cobbles, shouting out in excitement. His words were incomprehensible to me but I could see what he had on his arm. 'Look! Look!' he must have been saying. 'I have found a ladybird! Look!' But no one was interested. The adult in charge gasped at him to be careful, to slow down. Worry is a universal tongue.

147

At the top I ate fritters and fries and had a beer. I can do this. I did not miss Absentia at all. Far away the boats were hooting as they arrived and departed. I scanned the horizon with the binoculars but it was still too far away so I crept back down the cobbles to where ponies were still waiting to take the weary home to the harbour. I walked. Absentia would have liked it here. So I will like it here for her instead.

*

I do not subscribe to the tidy school of resolution. You could ask why she disappeared and I might say because I was not good enough, she was not kind enough, we were not close enough, that nothing was enough.

But that's absurd. Did you not talk? Didn't you ask? Didn't you try? Or did you vanish onto a high-altitude balcony without a word and shut out the world as you surveyed all life below through ten by fifty 'affordable excellence' binoculars? Yes. That is what I did.

I will go back of course and she will not be there because she has not been there for nine months. I do not know where she is. I have searched and searched for her. Every day I raise the glasses to my eyes and adjust the focus and bring images together and like a hawk hunting prey I square the land and like detectives in a post-mortem fingertip search I leave no blade of grass unexamined and still we are not reunited.

I have a map of my country and a map of Europe and a map of the world and a map of the heavens. I stare at them until I am dizzy, looking for clues. I do not know where I will go next. Somewhere there is a better balcony from which to search, up a staircase of a thousand steps, there must be narrower streets that twist more and more recklessly along which I can swoop and travel and search through thick lenses. The voices of strangers must be louder and shriller, have you seen my ladybird I will call, and the wise women selling corn on the cobs will look away from the crazed foreigner. Do not disturb the chickens.

Airports across the globe will be on alert for a woman disguised as a sunflower seedpod heading for Madagascar who

orders a full fried breakfast and then forgets her name and her
plans and her timescales and her itinerary, they will wonder at
the litter on her feet and an old man in a rocking chair will
share his rum and mango juice with her while reaching for his
cell phone to summon assistance from the elders of the village.

There is no time for this now. I am perched like a vulture on
the parapet. I drink beer. I eat a salami sandwich. The sun is
setting and the call is about to begin. I am at my best when I
do not understand.

Now in the dark the vista is different. I can spy
women taking in their washing from lines pushed out on
perilous poles above the streets, rugs and bedding, sheets and
pillowcases, duvets without patches, world without end.
Headlights sweep arcs into the skies and a light bulb slung
across the street on a cable sheds a pool of grimy yellow onto
bags of spilled rubbish. Cats slink in the gutters, look back,
sniff and sidle on.

Still the call comes. I was always faithful but up close
and personal was too close for comfort. I thought that
magnification from a distance was how it worked but when I
stretched out a hand you were miles gone and in a far-flung
fling. You were magnificent.

Elbows rest on the edge, binoculars are in position. A
grey-headed and wizened raven that ought to be in bed has
found a peach stone and is pinning it to the tile on the edge of
the balcony seven streets away with his gnarled foot while he
pecks at the fibres for a scrap of nourishment. It threatens to
roll off, he flaps and fits it into his mouth with difficulty,
shakes and rearranges himself and gets it under his claw again,
and starts pecking again. I watched until the great seedpod
rolled off and he flew away disgusted. I watched a man argue
with another man with a mobile phone in a hotel bedroom. I
watched the lights on the minarets and focussed my lenses on
the loudspeakers, willing them to start up again just for me.

Contributors

Ginny Baily is political editor of the *Africa Research Bulletin* and co-editor of Riptide. She has published stories and poems in numerous magazines. Her first novel, *Africa Junction,* is due from Harvill Secker in 2011.

Jane Feaver is a novelist and short story writer. *According to Ruth* (2007) was shortlisted for the Author's Club First Novel award and the Dimplex Prize. *Love Me Tender* was shortlisted for the Edge Hill Short Story Prize, 2010.

Sally Flint is a published writer of poetry and prose and co-editor of Riptide. She is a facilitator for 'Stories Connect', which helps ex-offenders and substance mis-users change their lives through literature.

Luke Kennard lectures in creative writing at the University of Birmingham. His second collection of poetry, *The Harbour Beyond the Movie,* was shortlisted for the Forward Prize in 2007. *The Migraine Hotel* was published in 2009.

Eleanor Knight has had stories published in *Retro Retro* (Serpent's Tail) and *Riptide* Vols. 2 and 4. She lives in Lewes and is working on a novel.

Jo Lloyd was the winner of the 2009 Asham Award and the 2009 Willesden Herald International Short Story Prize. Her stories have appeared in *Waving at the Gardener* (Bloomsbury), *New Short Stories 3* (Pretend Genius) and *Cut to the Bias*(Honno).

Alison MacLeod is Professor of Contemporary Fiction at the University of Chichester. She was awarded the Society of Authors' Olive Cook Award for Short Fiction. 'Café Bohemia' first appeared in *The Stinging Fly* (ed. Declan Meade).

Adam Marek was shortlisted for the *Sunday Times EFG Private Bank Short Story Award.* His story collection, *Instruction manual for swallowing,* was nominated for the Frank O'Connor Prize. He is working on his first novel. www.adammarek.co.uk

Alison Napier has had short fiction published in several anthologies and literary journals. She is currently working on a novel, *Take-Away People*. www.alisonnapier.co.uk

Jenny Newman has written two novels, *Going In* (Penguin) and *Life Class* (Arrow). Her short fiction has been broadcast on BBC Radio 4, and published in *The London Magazine*, *This Is* and *Pool*.

Wena Poon is a Singapore-born American writer. She has published a novel, *Alex y Robert* (Salt), and two short fiction collections *The Proper Care of Foxes* and *Lions In Winter*. In 2010 she won the Willesden Herald Short Story Prize.

Jane Rogers has written eight novels including *Mr Wroe's Virgins*, *Promised Lands*, and *The Voyage Home*. She was shortlisted in the BBC National Short Story competition 2009. She is Professor of Writing at Sheffield Hallam University.

Nicholas Royle is author of five novels and two novellas. His short story collection, *Mortality*, was shortlisted for the Edge Hill Prize. He teaches creative writing at Manchester Metropolitan University and runs Nightjar Press.

Jane Rusbridge teaches Creative Writing at the University of Chichester. *The Devil's Music*, her first novel, is described as 'a beautifully told story of family secrets and betrayal, involving knots, Harry Houdini and the shifting landscape of memory.'

Robert Shearman is an award-winning writer for stage, TV (*Dr Who*) and radio. *Tiny Deaths* (Comma Press) and *Love Songs for the Shy and Cynical* (Big Finish Books) won respectively the 2007 World Fantasy Award and the Readers' Prize, Edge Hill Short Story Award, 2010.

Karen Stevens is a Senior Lecturer in Creative Writing at the University of Chichester. She has recently completed her first novel, *The Bridge*, shortlisted for The Daily Mail Novel Writing Competition 2009.

Zoë Teale is a short story writer and novelist. *Sir Phoebus's Ma*, was published by Orion in 1995 and she is currently working on a new novel.

Matt Thomas is an American artist who lives and works in Devon. He can be contacted at evanonrev@yahoo.co.uk

Matt Thorne is the author of six novels including *Eight Minutes Idle* (winner of an Encore Award) and *Cherry* (long-listed for the Man Booker Prize.) He co-edited the anthologies *All Hail the New Puritans* and *Croatian Nights*.